"Do You Have Any Idea About The Extent Of My Craving For You?

How long it has gone unfulfilled? How much it has cost me to suppress it, to stay away from you?"

Each beat of her heart rocked her as a shadow detached itself from the darkness engulfing the upper floor, taking his form. His body materialized. Then his face emerged from the shadows and she gasped.

Even from this distance, there was no mistake.

The ultra-efficient surgeon, the indulgent benefactor, the teasing, patient playmate was gone. A man of tempestuous passions had emerged in his place.

And she had no right to his passion. She'd lose even the bittersweet torment of his nearness tomorrow. She'd never again feel this alive.

* * *

To find out more about Desire's upcoming books and to chat with authors and editors, become a fan of Harlequin Desire on Facebook www.facebook.com/HarlequinDesire or follow us on Twitter www.twitter.com/desireeditors!

Dear Reader,

I didn't set out to do it, but when I was halfway through writing *A Secret Birthright,* I realized that in it I'd gathered almost all of my most loved themes in writing for Harlequin Desire! A sheikh, a medical theme, a secret baby, family drama, royal intrigue, love at first sight and a seemingly impossible love.

Is it any wonder the result was one my most enjoyable books to write, ever?

As I wrote, unraveling the mysteries in the book, I loved being inside Fareed's mind as he finds out the secrets only as the reader does. I also loved being privy to Gwen's conflicted and anguished thoughts and emotions, which give us glimpses of the complex, high-stakes situation and let us wonder right along with her if, when it all comes to light, she will lose everything she's ever loved.

I hope you enjoy discovering the story's many secrets and accompanying Fareed and Gwen on their bumpy road to happy-ever-after as much as I enjoyed writing it all!

I love to hear from readers, so please feel free to contact me at oliviagates@gmail.com. I'd also love it if you "Like" my Olivia Gates author page on Facebook and follow me on Twitter @OliviaGates.

To find out about my latest releases, read excerpts and enter my contests, please visit me on the web at oliviagates.com.

Enjoy, and thanks for reading.

Olivia Gates

OLIVIA GATES

A SECRET BIRTHRIGHT

Harlequin®

Desire

Recycling programs
for this product may
not exist in your area.

ISBN-13: 978-0-373-73149-7

A SECRET BIRTHRIGHT

Copyright © 2012 by Olivia Gates

Recent books by Olivia Gates

Harlequin Desire

The Sarantos Secret Baby #2080
***To Touch a Sheikh* #2103
A Secret Birthright #2136

Silhouette Desire

**The Desert Lord's Baby* #1872
**The Desert Lord's Bride* #1884
*The Desert King #1896
†*The Once and Future Prince* #1942
†*The Prodigal Prince's Seduction* #1948
†*The Illegitimate King* #1954
Billionaire, M.D. #2005
In Too Deep #2025
  "The Sheikh's Bargained Bride"
**To Tame a Sheikh #2050
***To Tempt a Sheikh* #2069

*Throne of Judar
†The Castaldini Crown
**Pride of Zohayd

Other titles by this author available in ebook.

OLIVIA GATES

has always pursued creative passions like singing and handicrafts. She still does, but only one of her passions grew gratifying enough, consuming enough, to become an ongoing career—writing.

She is most fulfilled when she is creating worlds and conflicts for her characters, then exploring and untangling them bit by bit, sharing her protagonists' every heart-wrenching heartache and hope, their every heart-pounding doubt and trial, until she leads them to an indisputably earned and gloriously satisfying happy ending.

When she's not writing, she is a doctor, a wife to her own alpha male and a mother to one brilliant girl and one demanding Angora cat. Visit Olivia at www.oliviagates.com.

To all my Romance World friends.
Authors, editors, fans and reviewers.

I don't have enough words to thank you
for being who you are, and for being there for me
when I most needed friends.

One

"I don't want to see another woman. Ever again."

A long moment of silence greeted the fed-up finality of Sheikh Fareed Aal Zaafer's declaration. His companion's empathy and exasperation hung heavy in the stillness.

Then Emad ibn Elkaateb sighed. "I *am* almost resigned a woman isn't in the cards for you. But because this isn't about you or your inexplicable personal choices, I have to insist."

Fareed's laugh was one of incredulous fury. "What *is* this? *You,* who brought me damning proof on each imposter? You're now asking me to suffer another one? To grit my teeth through more pathetic, disgusting lies? Just who are you and what have you done with Emad?"

Suddenly the decorum Emad maintained dissolved. Fareed blinked. Emad rarely budged in giving him the "dues of his birthright," insisted it was an integral part of *his* honor as Fareed's right-hand man to observe Fareed's position as his prince.

Now Emad's expression softened with the indulgence of twenty-five years of being closer to Fareed than his family, friends and staff in his medical center combined. "Anticipating your disappointment was the only reason I objected to the…scheme that brought upon you all of those opportunists. On any other account, I can't begin to fault your methods. My own haven't produced results either. Hesham hid too well."

Fareed gritted his teeth on the upsurge of frustration and futility. Of grief.

Hesham. The sensitive soul and exceptional artist. And out of Fareed's nine siblings, the youngest brother and the most beloved.

It was their father and king's fault that Hesham had hidden. Over three years ago, Hesham had returned from a long stay in the States to announce that he was getting married. He'd made the mistake of believing their father might be persuaded to give him his blessing. Instead, the king had flared into an unprecedented rage. He'd forbidden Hesham to contact his fiancée again, or to consider wedding anyone not chosen by their royal house.

When Hesham refused to obey him, the king's fury had escalated. He'd ranted that he'd find the American hussy who'd tried to insinuate herself into the royal line and make her wish she'd never plotted to ensnare his son. As for Hesham, he wasn't letting him dabble in his pointless artistic pursuits and shirk his royal duties anymore. This was no longer about what or whom Hesham chose to amuse himself with. This was about heritage. He wouldn't let him taint their bloodline with an inferior union. Hesham *would* obey, or there would be hell to pay.

Fareed and his brothers and sisters had intervened on

their brother's behalf, then had worked together to release him when their father had placed Hesham under house arrest.

Hesham had wept as he'd hugged them and told them he had to disappear, to escape their father's injustice and to protect his beloved. He'd begged for their word that they'd never look for him, to consider him dead, for all of their sakes.

None of them had been able to give that word.

But even though each had tried to keep track of him, with Fareed the one who'd gone to the greatest lengths, Hesham had all but erased himself from existence.

A new wave of rage against their father scorched his blood.

If it hadn't been for the oath he'd taken to serve his people, he would have left Jizaan, too. But that wouldn't have been a punishment for their father. He wouldn't have cared about losing another son. All he'd said after Hesham's disappearance had been that he cared only that Hesham did nothing to disgrace their family and kingdom. Fareed believed that their father would have preferred to see Hesham and any of his future children dead before that came to pass.

What had come to pass had been even worse.

After years of Fareed yearning for any contact with him, Hesham's call came from an E.R. in the States. Hesham had called him only to use his last breaths to beg for a favor. Not for himself, but for the woman for whom he'd left his world, who'd *become* his world.

Take care of Lyn, Fareed...and my child...protect them...tell her she's everything...tell her...I'm sorry I couldn't give her what she deserves, that I'll leave her alone with...

There'd been no more words. He'd almost bloodied his

throat roaring for Hesham to tell him more, to wait for him to come save him. He'd heard only an alien voice, telling him his brother had been taken to surgery.

He'd flown out immediately, dread warring with the hope that he'd be in time to save him. He'd arrived to find him long dead.

Learning that Hesham had been in no way responsible for the accident had deepened his anguish. An eighteen-wheeler had lost control and decimated eleven cars, killing many and injuring more. Grief had compromised his sanity, yet he'd fought it to offer his services. As an internationally recognized surgeon and one of the leading experts in his field, he had been gratefully accepted, and he'd operated on the most serious neurological injuries, had saved other victims as he hadn't been able to save Hesham.

It had been too late by the time he'd learned that a woman had been with Hesham in the car. She'd had no injuries, no identification, and had left the hospital as soon as Hesham had died. Descriptions had varied wildly in the wake of the mass casualties.

With a bleeding heart, he'd taken Hesham's body back to Jizaan. After a heart-wrenching funeral, which the king hadn't attended, Fareed had launched a search for Lyn and the child.

But Hesham *had* hidden too well. It seemed he'd been erasing each step as he'd taken it. Investigations into the new identity he'd assumed had revealed no wife or child. Even the car he'd died in had been a rental under yet another name.

After a month of dead ends, Fareed had taken the only option left. If he couldn't find Hesham's woman, he'd let *her* find *him*.

He'd returned to where Hesham had died, placed appeals in all the media for the woman to contact him. He'd kept his message cryptic so only the right person would approach him. Or so he'd intended...

Women had *swamped* him.

Emad had weeded out the most blatant liars, like those with teenaged children or with none, and still advised Fareed not to waste his time on the rest. He'd been certain they'd all turn out to be fortune hunters. Being a billionaire surgeon and desert prince, Fareed had always been a target for gold diggers. And he'd invited them by the drove.

Fareed couldn't comply, couldn't let anyone who remotely answered the criteria go without an audience.

He'd felt antipathy toward every candidate before she'd opened her mouth. But he'd forced himself to see each performance to its exasperating end. He believed Hesham, the lover and creator of beauty, would have fallen in love only with someone flawless inside and out, someone refined, worthy and trustworthy. But what if Hesham hadn't been as discerning as he'd thought?

But after a month of agonizing letdowns, Fareed had gone home admitting his method's failure. He'd known any new attempt would fail without new information to use. For two more months, he'd been driven to the brink on a daily basis thinking his brother's flesh and blood was out there and might be in need.

He'd groped for a sanity-saving measure, answered a plea from a teaching hospital in the States to perform charity surgeries. A part of his schedule was always dedicated to charity work, but he'd never tackled so many within such a tight time frame. And his work at his own medical center was too organized to provide solace. For the last four weeks he'd lost himself in the grueling endeavor that had managed to anesthetize his pain.

Today was the last day. And after the distraction provided by the crushing schedule, he dreaded the impending release like an imminent jump off a cliff…

"Somow'wak?"

Emad's prodding "Your Highness" brought him out of his lapse into memories and frustration.

Fareed heaved to his feet. "I'm *not* seeing any more women, Emad. You were right all along. Don't go soft on me now."

"I assure you I'm not. I've been sending the women who've come asking for an interview with you away."

Fareed blinked. "There's been more?"

"Dozens more. But I interviewed them in your stead without inflicting even a mention of them on you."

Fareed shook his head. Seemed his desperate measure would haunt him for Ullah only knew how long. "So what's new now? Don't tell me you're suddenly hoping that my 'grief-blinded gamble' might, 'against all rationality and odds,' bear fruit?"

Emad's lips twitched at Fareed's reminder of his reprimands. *"Somow'wak* has an impeccable memory."

"Aih, it's a curse." A suspicion suddenly struck him. "Are you telling me you want me to start this…*farce* all over again?"

"I want you to see this one woman."

Fareed winced at the look that entered his eyes. Emad wouldn't look at a lion with more caution.

Jameel. Great. He was losing it. He huffed in disgust at his wavering stamina. "Why this one? Why is she special?"

Emad sighed, clearly not appreciating needing to explain his conviction. "Her approach was unlike any other. She didn't use the contact number you specified in the ad but has been trying to reserve an appointment with you through the hospital from the day we arrived. Today they told her that you were leaving and she started weeping...."

Fareed slammed down the dossier he'd picked up. "So she's even more cunning than the rest, realized that the others' approach hadn't borne fruit and tried to get past your screening by conning her way to me through my work. And when *that* didn't work, she made a scene. Is that why you want me to see her? Damage control? To stop compounding the 'scandal I created for myself and my family'?"

Emad's dark eyes emptied of expression. "I wouldn't want to resurrect that mess after I managed to contain it. But that's not why. The people in reception today are new. They only heard the story of her waiting around for the past four weeks in case you had an opening in your schedule from her disjointed accounts. When they couldn't deal with her, they sent for me, and I...saw her, heard what little she'd been able to say. She...*feels* different from the rest. Feels truly distraught."

Fareed snorted. "An even more superlative actress, eh?"

"Or maybe the real thing."

His heart boomed with hope, once, before it plummeted again into despondence. "You don't believe that."

Emad leveled his gaze on him. "The real thing *does* exist."

"And she doesn't want to be found," Fareed growled. "She must know I've turned the world upside down to find her and she didn't come forward. Why would she decide to show up when nothing has changed?"

"Maybe nothing we know of."

Fareed closed his eyes. Emad's calm logic was maddening him. He was in a far worse condition than he'd realized if anything Emad, of all people, said or did had him within a hair's breadth of going berserk. It seemed he'd distracted himself at the cost of pushing himself to a breakdown.

Emad's deep tones, so carefully neutral, felt like discordant nails against his restraint. "But what we do know is that Hesham's Lyn is still out there."

And what if that woman down there was her?

He closed his eyes against hope's insidious prodding. But it was too late. It had already eaten through his resistance.

This woman most probably wasn't; but really, what was one more performance to suffer? He'd better get this over with.

He opened his eyes as Emad opened his mouth to deliver another argument. He raised his hand, aborting it. "Send her up. I'm giving her ten minutes, not a second more. Tell her that. Then I'm walking out and I'm never coming back to this country."

Emad gave a curt nod, turned on his heels.

He watched him exit the ultramodern space the hospital had given him as his consultation room, before he sagged in the luxury of the leather swiveling chair. It felt as if he'd sunk into thorns.

If more fake, stomach-turning stories about his brother were flung in his face, he would not be responsible for his actions.

He glowered at the door. He'd seen all kinds. From the sniveling to the simpering to the seductive. He had an idea which type this one would be. The hysterical. Maybe even the delusional.

He steeled himself for another ugly confrontation as the door was pushed open. Emad preceded the woman into the room.

But he barely saw him. He didn't hear what Emad said before he left, or notice when he did.

All he saw was the golden vision approaching until only the wide desk stood between them.

He found himself on his feet without realizing he'd moved, only one thought reverberating in his mind.

Please, don't be Hesham's Lyn!

The thought stuttered to a standstill.

B'Ellahi, what was he thinking? He should be wishing that she was, that his search was over.

It shouldn't make a difference that her drowned sky-at-dawn eyes dissolved his coherence and the sunlight silk that cascaded over her bosom made his hands ache to twist in it. It didn't matter that the trembling of her lush lips shook his resolve and her graceful litheness gripped his guts in a snare of instant hunger. If she turned out to be Hesham's Lyn…

His thoughts convulsed to a halt again.

He wanted her to be anything *but* that. Even another imposter.

B'Ellahi, why?

The answer churned inside him with that desire that had surged out of nowhere at her sight.

Because Hesham's Lyn would be off-limits to him. And he wanted this woman for himself. He wanted her…

As he'd wanted her the first and only time he'd seen her.

He *remembered* her now!

It was the total unexpectedness of seeing her again, let alone here, that had thrown him at first. That, and the changes in her.

That time he'd seen her, her luminous hair had been scraped back in a severe bun. She'd been wearing makeup that he now realized had obscured her true coloring and downplayed her features. A dark suit of masculine severity had attempted to mask her screaming femininity.

She'd been younger, far more curvaceous, yet somehow less ripe. Her vibe had been cool, professional…until she'd seen him.

One thing remained the same. Her impact on him. It was as all-consuming as it had been when he'd walked into that conference room.

He vaguely remembered people scurrying to empty a place for him at the front row. She'd been at the podium. It wasn't until the stunning effect she'd had on him ebbed slightly that he realized what she'd been doing there.

She'd been delivering the very presentation he'd gone to that conference to attend, about a drug that helped regenerate nerves after pathological degeneration or trauma. He'd heard so much about the outstanding young researcher, the head of the R & D team. He'd had a mental image to go with her prodigious achievements, one that had collapsed under its own inaccuracy at the sight of her.

He'd held her gaze captive as he'd sat grappling with impatience for the presentation to be over so he could approach her, claim her. Only his knowledge that the sight of him had been as disruptive to her had mitigated his tension. His pleasure had mounted at seeing her poise shaken. She'd managed to continue, but her crisp efficiency had become colored by the self-consciousness he'd evoked. Every move of her elegant body and eloquent hands, every inflection of her cultured delivery, *everything* about her had made focusing on the data she'd been conveying a challenge. But her work had been even more impressive than he'd anticipated, only deepening his delight with her.…

"Is it all a lie? Are *you* a lie?"

He almost flinched. That red wine-and-velvet voice.

It had taken hearing it to know it had never stopped

echoing in his mind. Now it was made even more potent by the raggedness of emotion entwined in it.

But had she said…?

The next second her agitation cascaded over him, silencing questions and bringing every thought to a shocked halt.

"Is your reputation all propaganda? Just hype to pave the way to more reverence in the medical field and adulation in the media? Are you what your rare detractors say you are? Just a prince with too much money, genius and power, who makes a career of playing god?"

Two

Gwen McNeal heard the choking accusations as if they came from a disembodied voice. One that sounded like hers.

It seemed the past weeks had damaged what had been left of her sanity. She'd made her initial request for a meeting with it already strained. But as time had ticked by and her chances of meeting him had diminished, her stamina had dwindled right along.

She'd thought she'd be a mass of incoherence when she was finally in his presence.

Then she was there, and the sight of him had jolted through her like a lightning bolt. The intensity of his gaze, of his impact, had slashed the last tethers of her restraint.

She'd just accused him of being an over-endowed sadist who lived to make lesser beings beg for his intervention.

At least the unchecked flow had stopped. All she could

do now was stare in horror at him as he stared back at her in stupefaction. And realize.

He *was* what she remembered. Description-defying. Or there had to be new adjectives coined to describe his brand of virility and grandeur. Seeing him felt like being catapulted into the past. A past when she'd known where her life was heading. A life that had been derailed since she'd laid eyes on him.

Ever since, she'd told herself she'd exaggerated her memories of him, had built him up into what no one could possibly be.

But he was all that. It was all there, and more. The imposing physicality, the inborn grace and power, the sheer influence. She had no doubt time would continue to magnify his assets until he did become godlike.

One thing time hadn't enhanced, though. His effect on her. How could it when that had been shattering to start with?

Then he moved. The move itself was almost imperceptible, but the intention behind it, to come closer, when that would engulf her even deeper into his aura, intensify his effect, went off inside her like a clap of thunder.

Desperation burst from her in a new rush of resentment. *"Five minutes?* That's what you allow people in your presence? Then you walk away without looking back? Do you smirk in satisfaction as they run after you begging for a few more moments of your priceless time? Do you enjoy making them grovel? That's how much regard the world's leading philanthropist surgeon really has for others?"

A slow blink swept his sinful lashes down, before they lifted to level his smoldering gaze on her.

"I actually said ten minutes."

She'd thought his voice had been hard-hitting in the videos she'd seen of his interviews, lectures and educational surgeries. In reality, the depth and richness of his tones, the potency of his accent, the beauty of his every inflection made the words he uttered an invocation.

"And when I said that…"

She cut him off, unable to hear more of that spell. "So you granted me *ten* minutes instead of five. I can see how your reputation was founded, on such magnanimous offers. But I've already wasted most of those ten minutes. Do I start counting down the rest before you walk away as if I'm not here?"

He shook his head as if it would help him make sense of her words, and L.A.'s winter afternoon sun slanting through the windows glinted off his raven mane. "I won't do any such thing, Ms. McNeal."

Her heart gave one detonation. He…he…he *remembered* her?

The world receded into a gray vortex. A terrible whoosh yawned in her ears. Everything faded away as she plunged in a freefall of nothingness.

Something immovable broke her plummet, and she found herself struggling within the living cables that encompassed her, reaching back to the reprieve that oblivion offered.

"*B'Ellahi*…don't fight me."

The dark melody poured into her brain as she lost all connection with gravity, was swathed in hot hardness and dizzying fragrance. She opened her eyes at the sensation and that face she'd long told herself she'd forgotten filled her vision. She hadn't forgotten one line of symmetry or strength, one angle or slash or groove of nobility and character and uniqueness. Sheikh Fareed Aal Zaafer would be unforgettable after one fleeting look. Secondhand exposure would have been enough. But that firsthand encounter had been indelible.

But if she'd thought his effect from a distance the most disruptive force she'd ever encountered, now that she filled his arms, he filled her senses, conquered what remained of her resistance.

A violent shudder shook her. He gathered her tighter.

"Put me down, please." Her voice broke on the last word.

His eyes moved to her lips as soon as she spoke, following their movements. Blood thundered in her head at his fascination. His hands only tightened their hold, branding her through her clothing.

"You fainted." His gaze dragged from her lips, raking every raw nerve in her face on its way back up to her eyes.

She fidgeted, trying to recoup her scattered coordination. "I just got dizzy for a second."

"You *fainted*." His insistence was soft like gossamer, unbending as steel. "A dead faint. I had to vault over the desk to catch you before you fell face down over that table."

Her eyes panned to where she'd been standing by a large, square, steel-and-glass table. Articles were flung all over the floor around it.

Even though she'd never fainted in her life, no doubt formed in her mind. She had. And he'd saved her.

The bitterness that had united with tension to hold her together disintegrated in the heat of shame at her behavior so far. All she wanted was to burrow into his power and weep.

She couldn't. For every reason there was. She had to keep her distance at all costs.

He was walking to the sitting area by the windows as if afraid she'd come apart if he jarred her. What did was the solicitude radiating from him.

She pulled herself rigid in his hold. "I'm fine now... please."

He stopped. She raised a wavering gaze to his, found it filled with something...turbulent. Then it grew assessing, as if weighing the pros and cons of granting her plea.

Then he loosened his arms by degrees, let her slide in nerve-abrading slowness down his body. She swayed back a step as soon as her feet found the ground, and her legs wobbled under her weight, as if she'd long depended on him to support it. His hand shot out to steady her. She shook her head. He took his hand away, gestured for her to sit down, command and courtesy made flesh and bone.

She almost fell onto the couch, shot him a wary glance as soon as she'd sought its far end. "Thank you."

He came to tower over her. "Nothing to thank me for."

"Just for saving me from being rushed to the E.R., probably with severe facial fractures, or worse."

His spectacular eyebrows snapped together as if in pain, the smoldering coals he had for eyes turning almost black. "Tell me why you fainted."

She huffed. "If I knew that, I wouldn't have."

His eyes drilled into hers, clearly unsatisfied with her answer. "You're not alarmed that you did faint, at least you're not surprised. So you have a very good idea why. Tell me."

"It was probably agitation."

His painstakingly sculpted lips twisted. "You might be a renowned pharmaceutical researcher, Ms. McNeal, but I'm the doctor among us and the one qualified to pass medical opinions. Agitation makes you more alert, not prone to collapse."

He wouldn't budge, would he? She had to give him something to satisfy his investigative appetite so she could move on to the one subject that mattered. "It—it was probably the long wait."

He still shook his head. "Eight hours of waiting, though long, wouldn't cause you to be so exhausted you'd faint. Not without an underlying cause."

"I've been here since 4:00 a.m…" His eyebrows shot up in surprise. And that was before she added, "yesterday."

His incredulity shot higher, his frown grew darker. "You've been sitting down there for thirty-six hours?"

He suddenly came down beside her, with a movement that should have been impossible for someone of his height, his thigh whisper-touching hers as those long, powerful fingers, his virtuoso surgeon's tools, wrapped around her wrist to take her pulse. Her heartbeats piled up in her heart before drenching her arteries in a torrent.

He raised probing eyes to her. "Have you slept or even eaten during that time?" She didn't remember. She started to nod and he overrode her evasion. "It's clear you did neither. You haven't been doing either properly for a long time. You're tachycardic as if you've been running a mile." Was he even wondering why, with him so near? "You must be hypoglycemic, and your weak pulse indicates your blood pressure is barely adequate to keep you conscious. I wouldn't even need any of those signs to guide me about your condition. You look—depleted."

From meeting her haggard face in the mirror, she knew she made a good simulation of the undead. But having him corroborate her opinion twisted mortification inside her.

Which was the height of stupidity. What did it matter if he thought she looked like hell? What mattered was that she fixed her mistake, got on with her all-important purpose.

"I was too anxious to sleep or eat, but it's not a big deal.

What I said to you is, though. I'm sorry for…for my out-bursts."

Something flared in his eyes, making her skin where he still held her hand feel as if it would burst into flame. "Don't be. Not if I've done anything to deserve this…antipathy. And I'm extremely curious, to put it mildly, to find out what that was. Do you think I left you waiting this long out of malice? You believe I enjoy making people beg for my time, offer it only after they've broken down, only to allow them inadequate minutes before walking away?"

"No— I—I mean…no…your reputation says the very opposite."

"But your personal experience says my reputation might be so much manufactured hype."

Her throat tightened with a renewed surge of misery. "It's just you…you announced you'd be available to be approached, but I was told the opposite, and I no longer knew what to believe."

She felt him stiffen, the fire in his eyes doused in something…bleak. She'd somehow offended him with her attempts at apology and explanation more than she had with her insults.

But even if she deserved that he walked away from her, she couldn't afford to let him. She had to beg him to hear her out.

"Please, forget everything I said and let me start over. Just give me those ten minutes all over again. If afterward you think you're not interested in hearing more, walk away."

Fareed crashed down to earth.

He'd forgotten. As she'd lambasted him, as he'd lost himself in the memory of his one exposure to her, in his delight in finding her miraculously here, then in his anxiety when she'd collapsed, he'd totally forgotten.

Why he'd walked away from her that first time.

As she'd concluded her presentation and applause had risen, so had everyone. He'd realized it had been the end of the session when people had deluged him, from colleagues to grant seekers to the press. He'd wanted to push them all away, his impatience rising with his satisfaction as her gaze had kept seeking him, before darting away when she'd found him focused on her.

And then a man had swooped out of nowhere, swept her off her feet and kissed her soundly on the lips. He'd frozen as the man had hugged her to his side with the entitlement of long intimacy, turned her to pose for photos and shouted triumphant statements to reporters about the new era "their" drug would herald in pharmaceuticals.

He'd grabbed the first person near him, asked, "Who's that?"

He'd gotten the answer he'd dreaded. *That,* a Kyle Langstrom, had been her fiancé and partner in research.

As the letdown had mushroomed inside him, he'd heard Kyle announcing that with the major hurdle in their work overcome, there'd soon be news of equal importance: a wedding date.

The knowledge of her engagement had doused his blaze of elation at finding her, buried all his intentions. His gaze had still clung to her receding figure as if he could alter reality, make her free to return his interest, to receive his passion.

Just before the tide of companions had swept her out of sight, she'd looked back. Their eyes had met for a moment.

It had felt like a lifetime when the world had ceased to exist and only they had remained. Then she'd been gone.

He'd seen her again during the following end-of-conference party. The perverse desire to see her again even when it oppressed him had made him attend it. He'd stood there unable to take his eyes off her. She'd kept her gaze averted. But he'd known she'd been struggling not to look back. He'd finally felt bad enough about standing there coveting another man's woman that he'd left with the party at full swing.

He hadn't returned to the States again until Hesham.

He'd replayed that last glance for months afterward. Each time seeing his own longing and regret reflected in her eyes. And each time he'd told himself he'd imagined it.

He'd long convinced himself he had imagined everything. Most of all, her unprecedented effect on him.

It had taken him one look today to realize he'd completely downplayed it. To realize why he'd been unable to muster interest in other women ever since. He might not have consciously thought it, but he'd found no point in wasting time on a woman who didn't inspire the white-hot recognition and attraction this woman had.

Now she'd appeared here, out of the blue, had been waiting to see him for a month, her last vigil lasting a day and a half of sleepless starvation. She'd just said she was here because he'd "announced he'd be available to be approached."

Had she meant his ad? Could it be, of all women, this one he'd wanted on sight, hadn't only been some stranger's once, but Hesham's, too?

If she had been, *he* must have done something far worse than what she'd accused him of in her agitation. What else would that be but some unimaginably cruel punishment of fate?

He hissed, "Just *tell* me and be done with it."

She lurched as if he'd backhanded her. No wonder. He'd sounded like a beast, seconds away from an attack.

Before he could form an apology, she spoke, her voice muffled with tears, "I lied—" She had? About what? "—when I said ten minutes would do. I *did* keep asking reception for any moments you could spare when they said full appointments were reserved for patients on your list. I now realize they couldn't have acted on your orders, must have done the same with the endless people who came seeking your services. But I was told you're leaving in an hour, and that long might not do now either and…"

He raised his hands to stem the flow of her agitation, his previous suspicions crashing in a domino effect.

"You're here for a *consultation?*"

She raised eyes brimming with tears and…wariness? Nodded.

Relief stormed through him. She wasn't here about the ad, about Hesham. She was here seeking his surgical services.

Next moment relief scattered as another suspicion detonated.

"You're sick?"

Three

She *was* sick.

That explained everything. The only thing that made sense. Terrible sense. Her desperation. Her mood swings. Her fainting.

She had a neurological condition. According to her symptoms, maybe…a brain tumor. And if she'd sought him out, it had to be advanced. No one sought him specifically except in conditions deemed beyond the most experienced surgeons' skills. In neurosurgery, he *was* one of three on earth who'd made a vocation of tackling the inoperable, resolving the incurable.

But a month had passed since she'd first tried to reach him. Her condition could have progressed from minimal hope to none.

Could it be he'd found her, only to lose her again?

No, he wouldn't. In the past, he'd walked away from her, respecting the commitment she'd made. But disease, even what others termed terminal, *especially* that, was what he'd dedicated his life to defeating. If he could never have her, at least he would give the world back that vibrant being who'd made giving hope to the hopeless her life's work....

"I'm not sick."

The tremulous words hit him with the force of a bullet.

He stared at her, convictions and fears crashing, burning.

Had she said...? Yes, she had. But that could mean nothing. She'd already denied knowledge of why she'd fainted. She could still be undiagnosed, or in denial over the diagnosis she'd gotten, hoping he'd have a different verdict....

"It's my baby."

This time, only one thing echoed inside his head. *Why?*

Why did he keep getting shocked by each new verification that this woman had a life that had nothing to do with him? That she'd planned and lived her life without his being the major part of it?

Often he'd found himself overwhelmed by bitterness without apparent reason. He now admitted to himself what that reason had been. That he still couldn't believe she hadn't waited to find him, had accepted a deficient connection with someone else.

But that sense of betrayal was ridiculous, had nothing to do with reality. Her marriage *had* been imminent when he'd seen her. So why did it shock him so much that she had a baby, the normal outcome of a years-old union?

And that baby was sick. Enough to need his surgical skills.

His heart compressed as he realized the reason, the emotions behind her every word and tear so far. The same desperation he'd once felt, to save someone whose life he valued above his own.

How ironic was it that her intensely personal need for his purely professional services had made her finally seek him out?

He'd long given in to fate that had deemed that their paths diverged before they'd had the chance to converge. But to have her enter his life this way *was* a punishment, an injury. And he wasn't in any condition to take more of either.

If it had only meant his own suffering, he would have taken any measure of both. But he held his patients' lives under the steadiness of his hand, their futures subject to the clarity of his decisions. He couldn't compromise that.

Now he had to deal her the blow of refusing her baby's case. He would make sure her baby got the very best care. Just not his.

He inhaled a burning breath. "Ms. McNeal…"

As if feeling he'd let her down, she sat up, eyes blazing with entreaty. "I have Ryan's investigations with me, so maybe minutes will do. Will you take a look, tell me what you think?"

She only wanted his opinion? Didn't want him to operate on her baby? If so…

Again, as if she felt him relenting, she scrambled up. He noticed for the first time the briefcase and purse she'd dropped. All he'd seen had been her. In spite of everything, his eyes still clung to her every move, every nuance, and his every cell ached with long-denied impulses.

He saw himself striding after her, catching her back, plastering her body against his, burying his fingers in the luxury of her golden cascade of hair, sweeping it aside to open his lips over her warm, satin flesh. What he'd give for only one taste, one kiss…

She was returning, holding the briefcase as if it contained her world, her dawn-sky eyes full of brittle hope.

Ya Ullah, how was beauty like that even possible?

He'd never been attracted to blondes, never preferred Western beauty. But to him, she was the embodiment of everything that aroused his wonder and lust. And it was only partially physical. The connection he felt between them, that which needed no knowledge or experience, just *was,* was everything he wanted. When he couldn't have her.

She started fumbling with the briefcase's zipper as she neared him, and another idea occurred to him.

If this would be only a consultation, he owed her a full one after all the suffering she'd endured for the mere hope of it.

He should also give himself a dose of shock therapy. Seeing her with her baby, with her whole *family,* might cure him of this insidious malady he'd been struck with at her sight.

He stayed her hand with a touch, withdrew his as if contact with her burned him, and before he tugged her against him.

"I won't be able to give you an opinion based on those investigations. I don't rely on any except those done to my specifications." Alarm flared in her eyes. He couldn't believe the effect her distress had on him. It...physically hurt. He rushed to add, "Anyway, my preferred and indispensable diagnostic method is a clinical exam. Is your baby downstairs with his father?"

Her gaze blipped, and she barely suppressed a start.

Before he could analyze her reaction, she murmured, her voice deeper, huskier, "Ryan is with his nanny at our hotel. They both got too tired and Ryan was crying nonstop and disturbing everyone, I had to send them away."

Agitation spread across her features like a shadow. "I thought I'd bring them back as soon as I got an appointment with you. But the hotel's near the airport, and at this time of day, even if I'd told Rose to come as soon as I knew you'd see me, it would have taken her too long to get here. I didn't even tell her, because Mr. Elkaateb said you had only minutes to spare. That's why I said an hour won't do…."

He raised a hand, stopped her anxiety in its tracks. "I'm going home on my private jet, so the timing of my departure is up to me. Call your nanny and have her bring Ryan over."

Her eyes widened. "Oh, God, thank you…"

A hand wave again stopped her. He hated the vulnerability and helplessness gratitude engendered in others, was loathe to be on its receiving end. Hers took his usual discomfort to new levels.

She nodded, accepting that he wanted none of it, dived into her purse for her phone.

In moments, with her eyes fixed on him, she said, "Rose…" She paused as the woman on the other side burst out talking. Realizing he must hear the woman, Gwen shot him an apologetic, even…shy glance. "Yes, I did. Get Ryan here ASAP."

He barely stopped himself at a touch of her forearm. "Tell her to take her time. I'll wait."

The look she gave him then, the beauty of her tremulous smile, twisted another red-hot poker in his gut. He had to get away from her before he did something they'd both regret.

He turned away, headed back to the desk and blindly started gathering the files he'd scattered.

When she ended her phone call, without looking up he asked the question burning a hole in his chest, trying to sound nonchalant, "Isn't your husband coming? Or is he back home?"

He *needed* to see her with her husband. He had to have that image of her with her man burned into his mind, to erase the one he had of her with *him*.

She didn't answer him for what felt like an eternity. His perception sharpened and time warped with her near.

He forced himself to keep rearranging the desk, didn't raise his eyes to read on her face the proof of her involvement with another. He should, to sever his own inexplicable and ongoing one. He couldn't. It would be bad enough to hear it in her voice as she mentioned her husband, the father of her child.

When her answer finally came, it was subdued, almost inaudible. He almost missed it. Almost.

His heart kicked his ribs so hard that he felt both would be bruised. His eyes jerked up to her.

She'd said, "I don't have a husband."

He didn't know when or how he'd crossed the distance back to her. He found himself standing before her again, the revelation reverberating in his head, in his whole being.

He heard himself rasp, "You're divorced?"

She escaped his eyes, the slanting rays of sunset turning hers into bottomless aquamarines. "I was never married."

He could only stare at her.

A long moment later, he voiced his bewilderment. "I thought you were engaged when I saw you at that conference."

He thought, indeed. He'd thought of nothing else until he'd forced himself into self-inflicted amnesia.

Color rushed back into her cheeks, making his lips itch to taste that tide of peach. "I was. We...split up soon afterward." She snatched a look back at him, her lips lifting with a faint twist of humor. "Sort of on the grounds of irreconcilable scientific differences."

Suddenly he felt like putting his fist through the nearest wall.

B'haggej' jaheem…in the name of *hell!* He'd walked away because he'd believed she would marry that Kyle Langstrom. And she *hadn't.*

Frustration charred his blood as realizations swamped him, of what he'd wasted when he hadn't pursued her, hadn't at least followed up on her news. He would have found out she hadn't married that…that *person.* But that didn't necessarily mean that…

"He's not the father of your child?"

She ended that suspicion with a simple, "No."

Before delight overtook him, another realization quashed it.

She might not have married Langstrom, but she had a man in her life. He *had* to know. "Then who is your child's father?"

She shrugged, unease thickening her voice. "Is this about Ryan's condition? Do you think knowing his father is important for managing it or for his prognosis?"

He was tempted to say yes, to make it imperative for her to answer him. The temptation passed, and integrity, damn it to hell, took over. He exhaled his frustration with the code he could never break. "No, knowing the source of a congenital malformation has no bearing on the course of treatment or prognosis."

"Then I don't see how bringing up his father is relevant."

She didn't want to talk about this. She was right not to. He'd never dreamed of pursuing private information from anyone, let alone the parent of a prospective patient. But this was *her,* the one woman he had to know everything about.

He already knew everything that was relevant to him. From her work, he'd formed a thorough knowledge of her intellect and capabilities. Instinct provided the rest, about her nature and character and their compatibility to his. What remained was the status of any personal relationship she might have.

And yet, there *was* a legitimate reason for him to ask about the father. "It's relevant because the father of your child should be here, especially if your child's condition is as serious as you believe. As his father, he has equal right to decide his course of treatment, if there is any, and an equal stake in his future."

Concession crept in her eyes. It was still a long moment later when she spoke, making him feel as if the words caused her internal damage on their way out. "Ryan... doesn't have a father."

And all he could ask himself now was when? When would that woman stop slamming him with shocks? When would she stop giving him fragments of answers that only raise more maddening questions?

"You mean he's not a part of your lives? Is he gone? Dead?"

What? the shout rang inside his head. *Just tell me.*

Her eyes shot up to his. She must be as attuned to him as he was to her. He'd kept his tone even, his demeanor neutral. But she must have sensed the vehemence of his frustration.

She finally exhaled. "I had Ryan from a donor."

This time he did stagger back a step.

There *was* no end to her surprises.

But he was beyond surprised. He was flabbergasted. He would have never even considered this a possibility.

Even though he knew this would mean something huge when he let it sink in, and he couldn't understand why she'd been so averse to disclosing this fact, it only raised more questions. "Why would someone so young resort to a sperm donor?"

She kept her eyes anywhere but at him, her color now dangerous. "Age is just one factor why women go the donor route. And it's been a while since I left the designation 'so young' behind. Thirty-two is hardly spring chick territory."

His lips twitched at this, yet another trace of wit. "With forty being the new thirty even where child bearing is concerned, you are firmly in that territory. If I'd just met you, I wouldn't give you more than twenty-two."

Her shoulders jerked on a disbelieving huff as she gave him one of those glances that made his blood pressure shoot up. "I've looked in a mirror lately, you know. You yourself said I look terrible. But anyway, thanks for the… chivalry."

"I only ever say what I mean. You have proof of that from my unsweetened interrogation." One corner of her lips lifted. "And my exact word was *depleted*. It's clear you're neglecting yourself in your anxiety over your child. It doesn't make you any less…breathtaking."

It was her own breath that stalled now. The sound it made catching in her throat made him dizzy with desire.

He intended to hear that sound, and many, many others, as he compromised her breathing with too much pleasure. For now he pressed on. "And I'll keep it up until you tell me the whole story, so how about you volunteer it?"

Her shoulders rose and dropped helplessly. "Maybe you should keep it up and I'll answer what I can because I don't know what constitutes a whole story to you."

"I want to know why a woman like you, who will be

pursued by men when you're *seventy*-two, chose to have a child without one. Was it because of your ex-fiancé? Was there more to your breakup than you let on? What did he do to put you off relationships?"

The hesitant humor playing on her lips reached her eyes. He couldn't wait until he could see it fully unleashed. "I did ask for it. But you can't be further from the truth in Kyle's case. I'm the villain of the piece in that story. It was because of me that even working together became counterproductive."

Zain. That was succinct and unequivocal. And still deficient.

He persisted, "Then why?"

She looked away again. "Not everything has to have a huge or complex reason. I just wanted a baby."

He knew she was hiding something. The conviction burned in his gut with its intensity. "And you couldn't wait to have one the usual way? When another suitable man came along?"

"I wasn't interested in having another man, suitable or not."

She fell silent. He knew she'd say no more on that issue.

He had more to say, to ask, to think, and everything to feel. It all roiled inside him, old frustrations and new questions. But one thing crystallized until it outshone everything else.

Not only didn't she have a man in her life, but she also hadn't wanted one. After she'd seen him. He *knew* it. Just like he hadn't wanted another woman after he'd seen her.

Elation swept him. Changed the face of his existence.

He didn't know how he stopped from doing what he'd wanted to do since that first moment—sweep her in his arms and kiss her until she begged for him. But he couldn't do it now.

Not having her now was still torment, only sweet instead of bitter, and the wait would only make having her in time that much more transfiguring.

For now, she needed his expertise, not his passion. He would give her everything she needed.

Her eyes were focused on him in such appeal that he could swear he felt his bones liquefying. "Won't you look at the investigations anyway, just to get an idea, while we wait?"

Eyes like these, influence like this, should be outlawed. He'd tell her that. Soon.

He smiled at her, took her elbow, guided her back to the couch. "I'd rather form an uninfluenced opinion."

She slid him a sideways glance, and the tinge of teasing there almost made him send everything to hell and unleash four years' worth of hunger on her. "Is anyone even capable of influencing your opinion?"

He laughed. For the first time…since he didn't remember when. After endless months of gloom, with her here, with her free, he felt a weight had lifted. If it weren't for Hesham, for his unfound woman and child, he would have said he was on the verge of experiencing joy.

"All this because of my interrogation?" He gently prodded her to sit down, got out his cell phone, called Emad and asked him to bring in a meal. When she insisted she'd settle for a hot drink, he overrode her with a gentle "Doctor's orders."

He came down beside her, close enough to feel imbued by the fragrant warmth of her body, but leaving enough space for her attempt to observe a semblance of formality.

She looked at him now, not enraged or wary or imploring, but with fascination, unable to stop studying him as he studied her, and the openness of her face, the clarity of her spirit…amazing.

He sighed his pleasure. "I would be a very poor scientist and a terrible surgeon if I wasn't open to new influences. I should be making the crack about you. After half an hour of my premium persistence all I got out of you was a half-dozen sentences."

She looked away, making him want to kick himself for whatever he'd done to make her deprive him of her gaze. "Your judgment *has* served you, and endless others, unbelievably well. You're one surgeon who deserves to have omnipotent notions."

"You mean my rare detractors aren't right and I'm not just a highborn lowlife suffering from advanced narcissistic sadism laced with a terminal god complex?"

She buried her face in her hands as he paraphrased her opening salvo, before looking back up at him, embarrassment and humor a heady mix in her eyes. "Do you think there's any chance you can pretend I never said that?"

He quirked his lips, reveling in taking her in degrees from desperation to ease. "Why would I? Because you were wrong? Are you sure you were? Maybe I behaved because you handed me my head."

A chuckle cracked out of her. "I doubt anyone can do that."

"You'd be really, really surprised what you can do."

He let *to me* go unspoken, yet understood.

Before he could analyze the effect this declaration had on her, Emad entered with the waitstaff.

Fareed saw the question, the hope in his eyes as Emad took in the situation. Fareed gave a slight headshake letting him know she wasn't the woman they'd been looking for.

But she was the woman *he'd* been looking for.

After preparing the table in front of them, and with disappointment and curiosity filling his eyes, Emad left.

For the next hour Fareed discovered new pleasures. Coddling Gwen—to her chagrin, before she succumbed, ate and drank what he served her, delighting in her re-surfacing steadiness, in the banter that flowed between them, the fluency of appreciation.

Then Emad knocked again. This time he ushered in a woman carrying a child. Gwen's child.

Fareed couldn't focus on either. He only had eyes for Gwen as she sprung to her feet, her face gripped with emotions, their range breathtaking in scope and depth. Anxiety, relief, welcome, love, protection and so much more, every one fierce, total.

He heard the child squeal as he threw himself into her eager embrace. He registered the elegant, classically pretty redhead in her late forties, who Gwen introduced as Rose Maher, a distant maternal relative and Ryan's nanny. He welcomed her with all the cordiality he could access, filed everything about her for later analysis. Then he turned to Gwen's child.

And the world stopped in its tracks.

Four

Fareed hadn't thought about Gwen's child until this moment. Not in any terms other than his being hers.

He hadn't had the presence of mind to formulate expectations, of the child, of his own reactions when he saw him. Had he had any mental faculties to devote to either, he would have thought he'd feel what he felt for any sick child in his care.

Now he knew anything he could have imagined would have been way off base.

She'd said Ryan didn't have a father. He could almost believe that declaration literally now. It was as if he was hers, and hers alone. Even the discrepancy in age and gender, the almost-bald head, did nothing to dilute the reality that he was a pure part of her, body and soul.

But that absolute kinship and similarity between child and mother wasn't why the sight of Ryan shook him to his core. Ryan, even though no more than nine or ten months old, was his own person. His effect wasn't an echo of his mother's, but all his own.

Ryan looked at him with eyes that were the same heavenly blue as his mother's but reflecting his own nature and character, inquisitive, intrepid, enthusiastic. His dewy lips were rounded on his same breath-bating fascination as he probed him as if asking if he was a friend. Then he seemed to decide he was, his eyes crinkling and his lips spreading.

"Say hello to Dr. Aal Zaafer, Ryan."

Fareed blinked as Gwen's indulgent tone cascaded over his nerves, such a different melody from any he'd heard from her.

It had an equal effect on Ryan, who smiled delightedly up at her. Next moment, his every synapse fired as the child turned back to him, encompassed him in the same unbridled smile. Then he extended his arms to him.

He stared at the chubby hands closing and opening, beckoning for him to hurry and pick him up.

Gwen moved Ryan out of reach. "Darling, the adorable act works only on me and Rose." Fareed's eyes moved from Ryan's crestfallen face to her apologetic one. "I didn't think he would ask you for a ride. He doesn't like to be held much, even by me. Too independent."

She thought his hesitation meant he didn't want to hold Ryan? She didn't realize he was just…paralyzed? Everything inside him wanted to reach back for Ryan, but the urge was so strong, so…unknown that it overwhelmed him.

He had to correct that assumption. He couldn't bear that she thought she'd imposed on him, couldn't stand seeing Ryan's chin quiver at being apparently rebuffed.

"I'm—" he cleared his throat "—I'm honored he thinks

I'm worthy of being his ride. He probably fancies one from a higher altitude."

A chuckle came from his left. His gaze moved with great effort from the captivating sight mother and son made to Rose.

She was still eyeing him with that almost-awed expression in her green eyes, but humor and shrewdness were taking over. "Ryan is a genius, and he knows a good proposition when he sees it. And you're as good as it gets."

A strangled gasp issued from Gwen. He didn't need to look at her to know that her eyes were shooting daggers at Rose.

His lips spread in his widest smile in years. "Ms. Maher, I knew you were a discerning woman the moment I saw you."

Rose let out a tinkling laugh. "Call me Rose, please. And oh, yes, I've been around long enough to know premium stuff when I see it, too."

He almost felt the heat of mortification blasting off Gwen. And he loved it. Rose was saying the exact things to dissolve the tension, to set him free of the immobility that had struck him.

"I am honored you think I belong on the premium shelf, Rose, almost as much as I was to be considered a desirable ride by Ryan." He shared another smile with the woman he already felt would be his ally, before he turned to Gwen and held out his arms.

His heart revved at what flared in her eyes. Momentary belief that his arms where inviting *her* into their depths. And a stifled urge to rush into them.

He let her know he'd seen it with a lingering glance before he transferred his smile to the baby who was already bobbing in her arms, demanding to be released. "Shall we, young sir?"

Ryan squealed his eagerness, reached back to him. Fareed noted his movements, already assessing his condition. He received him with as much care as he would a priceless statue that might shatter if he breathed hard. He looked down on the angelic face that was regarding him in such open wonder and something fierce again shuddered behind his breastbone.

Ya Ullah. That baby boy wielded magic as potent as his mother, and both their brands of spells had his name on them.

"You won't dent him, you know?" Rose said.

He swept his gaze to her, his lips twisting. "It's that clear I'm scared witless of holding him?"

Rose let out another good-natured laugh. "Your petrified expression did give me a clue or two that your experience in handling tiny humans *is* nonexistent."

"You don't have kids?"

Gwen's soft question swept his gaze back to her. She looked…horrified that she'd asked it.

Satisfaction surged inside him. She needed to know his private details as much as he'd needed to know hers. Even though she was clearly kicking herself for asking, she *was* dying to know. If he had children, and therefore, a wife.

He'd thought his life wasn't conducive to raising a family, that he didn't have that innate drive to become a father. Now he knew the real reason why he'd never thought of having children. Because he'd never found a woman he wanted to have them with.

Now looking at her, holding her child in his arms, he did.

He looked down at Ryan, who was industriously trying to undo his shirt's top buttons, before he looked back at her, giving her a glimpse of what he felt, if not too much of it. She wasn't ready for the full power of his intentions.

Then he murmured, "I don't."

Her lashes fluttered down. But he felt it. Her relief.

Elation spread through him. "But I am an uncle many times over, through two of my sisters and many first cousins, to an assortment of boys and girls from ages one to fifteen."

Gwen raised her eyes back to his, and...*ya Ullah*. Although still guarded and trying to obscure her feelings, the change that had come over them since she'd walked in here, the warmth she couldn't fully neutralize, singed him. "I bet you're their favorite uncle."

He grinned at her. "You honor me with your willingness to waste money betting on me. But a waste it would be. 'Favorite Uncle' is a title unquestioningly reserved for Jawad, my second-eldest brother. We call him the Child Whisperer. All I can lay claim to is that I think they don't detest me. I've been too preoccupied for the span of their lives to develop any real relationship with them. I would have liked to, but I have to admit, when I'm around them, I wonder how their parents put up with their demands and distraction and still function. I wonder how they made the decision to have them in the first place."

Wisps of mischief sparked in her eyes. "So that's why you kept asking me why I had Ryan? Because you think your nephews and nieces are a noisy, messy time-suck, and that an otherwise sane adult can have a child only by throwing away logic and disregarding all cautionary tales?"

He raised one eyebrow at her. "You know you've just called me Uncle Scrooge, don't you?"

Rose burst out chuckling. "Busted."

Gwen spluttered qualifications, shooting reproach at Rose, and he aborted her protests with a smile, showing her he was offense-proof, especially by anything coming from her. "Don't take it back when you're probably right. Interacting with children has never been one of my skills."

The only child he'd loved having around and taking care of had been Hesham. But he'd been only eight years older. He hadn't had any relevant experience with children outside his professional sphere.

She made an eloquent gesture indicating how he was holding Ryan with growing confidence, picking up various articles for his inspection. "If it has never been, then you're capable of acquiring new skills on the fly."

He'd always been uncomfortable receiving compliments, feeling the element of self-serving exaggeration in each. But her good opinion felt free of ulterior motives, *and* was clearly expressed against the dictates of her good sense. To *him* it felt…necessary.

He transferred his smile from her to Ryan. "It's this little man who's making me look like a quick study. He's the one doing the driving here."

Rose nodded. "Ryan does that. Just one look and a smile and the world is his to command. Very much like his mother."

Gwen's eyes darkened on something that gripped his heart in a tight fist. Something like…anguish. *Ya Ullah,* why?

Next second, he wanted to kick himself. How could he have forgotten the reason she was here? Ryan's condition.

But he had forgotten, during the lifetime since she'd walked in and turned his life upside down all over again. But from holding Ryan, he had a firm idea what his condition was. It was time he did everything he could to put her mind to rest about it.

He adjusted his grip on Ryan, feeling as if he'd always held him, turned his face up with a finger beneath the dimpled chin that was a replica of Gwen's. "Just so I don't look like a total marionette, Ryan, how about we pretend I have a say here? How about you let me examine you now?"

"How about I leave you to your new game and go find me some food?" Rose said, clearly to give them privacy.

Fareed produced his cell phone, called Emad back. Emad appeared in under ten seconds, as if he'd been standing behind the door, which he probably had been. Eavesdropping?

He was resigned that Emad would go to any lengths to ascertain his safety. But what was there to worry about here? Getting ambushed by lethal doses of charisma and cuteness?

He gave him a mocking glance that Emad refused to rise to. "Will you please escort Rose to an early dinner, Emad? And do make it somewhere where they serve something better than the food simulations you got us from the hospital's restaurant."

He expected Emad to obey with his usual decorum, which never showed if he appreciated the chore or not. But wonder of wonders, after nodding to him with that maddening deference, he turned to Rose with interest—almost eagerness—sparking in his eyes. Fareed hadn't seen anything like that in the man's eyes since his late wife.

The gregarious Rose eyed him back with open appreciation and murmured to Gwen for all to hear, "So incredible things *do* come to those who wait, eh, sweetie?" She didn't wait for Gwen's reaction and turned to Fareed. "It's been a treat meeting you, Sheikh Aal Zaafer. Take care of my lovelies, hmm?"

He bowed his head. "Fareed, please. And we'll be meeting again. *And* you can count on it."

She grinned at him, gave Gwen's hand a bolstering squeeze, caressed Ryan's cheek then gave *his* an affectionate pat before turning to Emad. "Shall we, Mr. Dark Knight?"

Emad gaped at her, clearly unable to believe this woman had just petted his prince. And that she'd called *him* that.

Then his eyes narrowed on a flare of challenge and approval as he gave her his arm. "By all means, Ms. Maher."

"Can't come up with a slogan for me, huh?" Rose beamed up at Emad. "But we have time. You'll think of something."

Before the door closed behind them, he heard Emad saying, "I don't need time, Ms. Wild Rose."

Fareed shook his head as the door closed behind them. He looked at Ryan, who was testing his stubble. "Can you believe this, Ryan? Emad teasing? Seems the power to change the laws of nature runs in your family."

Ryan squeaked as if in agreement and Fareed turned his gaze to Gwen, offered her his hand.

She stared at it for moments, her lower lip caught in her teeth, the very sight of conflicted temptation.

Before he gave in and reached for her hand, she gave it to him. He almost groaned and barely kept from bringing her nestling into him. He would make her give in, fully, irreversibly. In good time.

First, he would see to her peace of mind.

He made it a pledge. "Now I'll see to Ryan, Gwen."

Gwen's heart gave another boom before resuming its gallop.

But it wasn't only hearing her name on his lips that caused this latest disturbance. It was that he pronounced it *Gwaihn*, the breathy sound as he prolonged it a scorching sigh, making an intimacy of it, a promise...of so many things she couldn't even contemplate.

As if having her hand engulfed in his wasn't enough.

But she had herself to blame for this. She'd given her hand to him when she should have shown him she'd allow only formal interaction.

But she hadn't been able to withhold it. He was offering her what she'd been starving for. Support, strength other than her own to draw on, an infinite well of it. And whatever the consequences, she hadn't been able to stop from reaching for it.

He took them to the other end of the room, behind an opaque glass partition, to what turned out to be a fully fitted exam room.

"Gwen…" She started again. He cocked his head at her. "May I call you Gwen?"

She almost cried out, *No, you may not. Please, don't.*

Out loud she reluctantly said, "If you like, Dr. Aal Zaafer."

"I like, very much. And it's Fareed."

This was getting worse by the second. "Er…all right, Dr. Fareed…or, uh, do you prefer Sheikh?"

"Just Fareed."

And wasn't that the truth. He *was* unique, as his name proclaimed him to be. She'd looked up its meaning long before…

She shook her head, trying not to let the memories deluge her. "I can't call you just…that."

"Rose did, without a second's hesitation."

"Rose, as you noticed, is…is…"

"Blessedly unreserved. You should follow her example because I won't be called anything else by you. We're not only colleagues—" before she could contest *that,* he pressed on "—working in complementary fields, but I owe a lot of my most positive results to your breakthrough. The drug you developed has been my most reliable postoperative adjuvant therapy for years."

She gaped at him, her heart flapping inside her chest with a mixture of disbelief and pride. "I didn't realize… didn't know…"

He gave her one of those earth-shaking smiles of his. "Now you do. And even though I'm getting impatient with your slowness in developing the other drug that should shrink tumors before surgery, I'll forgive you on the strength of the first one. So we have far more than enough grounds for at least a first-name basis."

His lips listed those acceptable reasons, but his eyes told her the truth. He *wanted* this intimacy, would have it.

But she *needed* formality to hide behind, to keep things in perspective. Otherwise…

No. No otherwise. If anyone was off-limits to her, it was Fareed Aal Zaafer. She'd better never forget that.

"How about that game? It's super-easy and a lot of fun."

The indulgent drawl, which he only produced while talking to Ryan, snatched her out of her latest plunge into turmoil.

She watched him lay Ryan down on the exam bed and hand him a reflex hammer and penlight to play with. He moved around, turning on machines, gathering instruments, all the time explaining what he was doing and naming everything and what they were for.

He was talking to Ryan because he must know she knew all that. And that he was explaining to a ten-month-old, without the least condescension, as if he believed it was never too early for Ryan to learn, as if he hoped Ryan would at least understand the consideration in his attitude, choked her up again.

When he returned to Ryan's side, she asked, "Won't you call your assistants?"

He cocked one eyebrow at her, teasing sparking the

fiery brown of his eyes. "You think I can't handle examining one highly cooperative tyke on my own?"

"Actually, I'm worried this is the calm before the storm. In previous visits, Ryan acted as if the doctors were torturing him."

His eyebrows shot up before he looked at Ryan. "But you won't do that to your obedient ride, will you? And I won't make it such a cheerless endeavor that you'll be driven to tears. You can even assist me, hold instruments, test and taste them to your heart's content. Between us, we'll make this a great game, Ryan."

His thoughtfulness, then the way he said *Rye-aan,* Ryan's similar-sounding Arabic name, lanced through her.

After receiving Ryan's gleeful endorsement, he moved to start prepping him. She moved, too, bumped into him.

Feeling his steadying hands on her shoulders made her jump back. "I—I'll just undress him."

He gave her a tiny squeeze before setting her free and turning to Ryan. "As Ryan's designated driver this afternoon, I think he'd want me to do the honors, right, Ryan?"

Sure enough, Ryan let out a squeal of agreement.

She stood back, every nerve buzzing as he undid Ryan's snap-button jumpsuit with great care and dexterity, although it was clear he'd never performed the task before. Instead of fidgeting as he usually did, Ryan stunned her by chewing on a chart and offering Fareed every cooperation in stripping him down to his diapers.

"You're an extremely well-cared-for little prince, eh, Ryan?"

Her heart gave another painful thud, which was stupid. It was just a figure of speech.

"Now, let's start the game."

She stood mesmerized, watching Fareed's beautiful hands probe Ryan's muscles for power, pushing and pulling on his feet and legs, making Ryan an eager participant. He turned to sensation, walking his fingers along nerve paths, before pouncing with tickles and eliciting Ryan's shrieking giggles.

Next came recording muscle contraction and nerve conduction and he made Ryan help him fit in plugs and place leads over his body, all the time explaining everything. Ryan hung on his every word, his eyes rapt as he watched this larger-than-life entity who'd entered and filled his limited world. Fareed warned him that the tests were a bit uncomfortable, but would be over in no time, and Gwen braced herself for the end of the honeymoon.

But as he started the tests, instead of the dreaded wails, Ryan seemed to only notice Fareed's banter, awarded him with a steady stream of corroborating gurgles.

She shouldn't be surprised. Fareed's darkest silk voice made *her* forget a world outside existed, or a past or a future. . . .

What was she *thinking?* She should only be thinking of running away once this exam ended, forgetting she'd ever seen him again.

She'd only sought him as a last resort, had hoped to slip in among his appointments undistinguished. But she'd ended up having his attention in its most undiluted form. Then it had gotten worse and he'd remembered her, had been treating her since as if he...

Her thoughts piled up as he dressed Ryan then caught her eye. "I'll see those investigations now."

She pounced on the briefcase, but he gently stopped her fumbling, took over. He studied the X-rays and MRIs briefly, set aside the reports without reading them before putting everything back in the briefcase. Then he turned to Ryan, who was demanding to be picked up—by him.

He complied at once. "So how was that? Fun as I promised, eh?" Ryan whooped an agreement. "But you know what? We had all this fun together, and I haven't even introduced myself. My name is Fareed." He pointed to himself, said his name a few time.

Ryan's eyes twinkled before he echoed triumphantly, "Aa-eed."

"Ma azkaak men subbi!" Fareed exclaimed. "What a clever boy you are." Ryan seemed delighted by Fareed's approval, and continued to say Aa-eed over and over. Fareed guffawed. "We'll work on the *F* and *R* later. I bet you'll get it right in a couple of months, being a genius, like Rose said—" he turned to her "—and like your mother is."

Gwen felt about to faint again.

It's dreading his still-unvoiced verdict, she told herself.

But it wasn't. She *was* terrified of having her worst fears validated, but that lightheadedness, as if she'd been hungry all her life, was the effect he had on her. Anything he did, every move and look and breath induced pure emotional and erotic tumult....

What was happening to her? What was it about him that made her someone she didn't know? Someone who couldn't complete a thought without it turning into something...licentious?

He was guiding her back into the room, stopping by the desk for a computer tablet. At the sitting area, he set Ryan on the ground, gave him every safe article around to play with. Ryan instead made it clear he wanted to nap. She produced a blanket from the bag Rose had left behind and Fareed spread it in front of the couch, where Ryan crawled and promptly feel asleep facedown.

Once they sat down, Fareed said, "Tell me about Ryan, Gwen."

Don't call me that, she wanted to cry out. She needed to

regain her balance and there was no hope she would when he kept calling her *Gwaihn* in that lion's purr of his.

Instead she nodded her shaky assent. Over the next minutes, he obtained an exhaustive history of Ryan's pre- and postnatal periods and developmental milestones, his fingers flying over the glossy tablet's surface documenting it all.

Finally, he put the tablet down, turned to face her. "You do know he has *spina bifida occulta?*"

His question/declaration felt like a direct blow to her heart. She'd known, but had still been hoping against hope....

Tears surged again as she nodded. "As a researcher of drugs targeting the nervous system, I knew the basics of the condition." Incomplete closure of vertebrae around the spinal cord, which instead of hanging loose in the spinal canal was tethered to the bone, potentially causing varying degrees of nerve damage and disability. "I studied it extensively because I suspected Ryan of having it. But every pediatrician and neurologist told me not to worry, that ten percent of people have it and are asymptomatic, something they discover as adults during X-rays for unrelated complaints. I persisted, and a couple conceded that he has minor neurological deficits, which might or might not mean future disability but that there was no treatment anyway. But I couldn't just wait until Ryan grew up and couldn't walk or never developed bowel or urinary continence. I had to know for sure that there was nothing to be done, and only you...only your opinion will do..."

The sobs that had been banked broke loose.

He was down on his haunches in front of her in a blink, his hands squeezing her shoulders. "It was amazing that you noticed the mild weakness in his legs and clawing in his toes. He's sitting and crawling, and with him far away from being toilet-trained and without previous experience with children, I'm beyond impressed that you discerned his condition even after the repeated dismissal of your worries. But I can excuse the doctors who examined him. It would take someone as extensively versed in the rare as I am to form an opinion on so irregular a condition."

Her sobs had been subsiding gradually, at his soothing and under the urge to swamp him with questions.

The paramount one burst from her. "And you've formed one?"

He nodded. "You were absolutely right. Without surgery, he may develop increasing disability in lower limb motor function and bowel and urinary control."

She sank her fingers into his sinew and muscle. "So there is a surgery? To prevent further damage? What about any that already exists? *Is* there damage? What about bowel and urinary problems? My sources say even when surgery successfully closes the defect and releases the cord, those usually never go away...." She faltered on the last question, what she of all people knew was a long shot. "And if there's a residual handicap, would my drug help?"

He rose, came down beside her. This time, she sank into his solicitude gratefully, only the last vestiges of her willpower stopping her from physically seeking it.

"Most, if not all, surgeons wouldn't touch a case like Ryan's. They'd say their findings are too ephemeral to warrant a surgery that wouldn't offer much, if any, improvement. But I say different."

Hope surged so hard inside her that she choked with its agonizing expansion. "You—you mean you're not telling me to give up?"

He shook his head. "Of course, any surgery comes with risks." The world darkened again. He caught her hand, squeezed it. "I have to mention risks because it's unethical to promise you a risk-free procedure, not because I expect problems. But I can and do promise you and Ryan the best result possible."

Her tears faltered. "Y-you mean *you* want to operate on him?"

He nodded. "He'll be safe with me, Gwen."

She stifled another heart-wrenching sob. Fareed's arm slid around her. "And yes, your drug will regenerate the nerve damage. I know it's not approved for use on children, but because I believed the delay in approval was built on bureaucracy and not medical facts, I have obtained permission from the region's drug administration under my personal responsibility and have used it on even younger patients than Ryan with adjusted doses and certain precautions to astonishing results. Together, we'll cure Ryan, Gwen."

And she had to ask the rest, everything, now, before this turned out to be a deranged dream, before she fainted again. "How long will it take? The surgery? The recuperation? How soon can he have it? How much will it all cost?"

"The surgery itself is from four to six hours, and the recuperation is from four to six weeks. He can have it as soon as I prepare everything. And it won't cost a thing."

That stopped the churning world. Her tears. Her heart.

"You must have misunderstood," she finally whispered. "I'm not here seeking charity. I didn't even think of asking you to perform the surgery, only hoped you'd write me a report stating that it's a surgical case, so no surgeon could tell me it isn't."

He pursed his lips. "First, there's no charity involved—"

She struggled to detach herself from the circle of his support. "Of course there is. You're here performing pro bono surgeries. But I can pay. Just tell me how much, and I will."

"*You* will pay? Not that it's an issue here, but why wouldn't your insurance cover your child's medical expenses?"

She should be more careful what she said. He noticed everything. Now she had to satisfy him with an explanation or he'd corner her with demands for more information she couldn't give. "I insisted on costly investigations the doctors said weren't needed, moving me to an unfavorable insurance category, so the coverage would be only partial now. But that doesn't matter. I'm very well paid and I have a lot of money."

He leveled patient eyes on her. "Of course you are and you do. And there is *still* no cost involved."

She shook her head. "I can't accept a waiver of your fee. And then there are many other expenses besides that."

His lips quirked, teasing, indulgent. "First, I'm a big boy, if you haven't noticed, and I can waive my fee if I want to, which I mostly do. My 'reputation' isn't *totally* hype, you know. Second, there won't be any other expenses back home."

She gaped at him. For a full minute.

She finally heard a strangled echo. "Back home?"

He rose to his feet with a smile. "Yes. You, Ryan and Rose are coming with me to Jizaan."

Five

Gwen stared at the overwhelming force that was Fareed Aal Zaafer, and was certain of one of two things.

Either she'd finally lost her mind, or he was out of his.

She squeezed her eyes shut, as if that would stop the disintegration of this situation, set it back in the land of the acceptable. She opened her eyes again hoping she'd see on his face what should have been there from the start, polite forbearance with a patient's hysterical mother.

But he was looking at her with that indulgent intensity that singed her. Worse, a new excitement was entering his gaze, as if he was realizing more benefits to his decision by the second.

"As soon as Rose and Emad return, we'll go to your hotel and collect your luggage on our way to the airport. We'll be in Jizaan in under twenty-four hours."

He'd said it again. This Jizaan thing. She hadn't imagined it the first time. This was real. He meant it.

But he *couldn't* mean it. He had to be joking. He did have a wicked sense of humor....

No. His humor, while unpredictable and lightning-fast, was not in any way mean, at least, not in any of the lectures and interviews she'd seen. It would be beyond cruel to joke now and he was the very opposite of that: magnanimous, compassionate, protective.

But he was also single-minded and autocratic and she had to stop him before this crazy idea became a solid intention.

He detailed said intention. "We'll go to dinner first, or we can have it on board the jet." He got out his cell phone, cocked his head at her. "What would you like to have? Real food this time, I promise. I can either reserve seats in a restaurant, or have your choice ready on the jet."

"I can't go to your kingdom!"

The shaky statement managed to do the job. It stopped him short.

For about a second. Then he smiled. "Of course, you can."

She raised her hands. "Please, let's not start another 'I can't' 'No, you can' match. We just finished one about payment."

"Yes, let's not. You do remember how you fared in that last match? No point in repeating the same method and expecting different results, hmm?"

The definition of insanity, which also described this situation. She did feel her sanity slipping another notch. "You know what you're proposing is impossible."

"I know no such thing."

She shook her head, disbelief deepening, dread taking root. "You're asking me to just haul everyone halfway across the world...."

"I'll do the 'hauling,' so cross that out on your no-doubt

alphabetized list of worries. I'm sure you have your affairs sorted out for as long as you thought would see Ryan's medical situation resolved. But in case you're not fully covered, and fear repercussions for prolonged or unexcused absence from work, one phone call from me should get you an open-ended leave, with pay."

Her breathing had gone awry by the time he finished. "It's not just my work, it's...*everything*."

He crossed his arms over his chest, someone who would not be denied, who had an answer to everything. "Like what?"

She groped for something, anything, latched on the first logical thing that occurred to her. "Like passports. We didn't bring them on a trip we couldn't have dreamed would take us outside the States."

His daunting shoulder rose and fell. "You won't need them to enter my kingdom."

"But we'd need visas...."

He intercepted that, too. "Not when you're entering the kingdom with me, you don't. And I'll bring you back with me, so you won't need more than your American IDs to re-enter the States."

Her eyes darted around, as if looking for a way out. There was none. He kept neutralizing possible objections in advance. "And anyway, to make you feel better, once in Jizaan, I'll have the American embassy there issue new passports for you and I'll have visas stamped on them."

She knew he could do that with a flick of a finger. Any country would bend over backward to accommodate him.

"And if you're worried about your family, I'll call them right now, give them all my contact info, so they'd be in touch with you at all times. I can even take any of them who wish to come along, too."

Her heart emptied at his mention of her family. A subject she had to close before he probed it open. "Rose is my closest relative."

And probe he did. "You said she was a maternal relative. So what happened to your mother?"

She could feel the familiar pain and loss expanding all over inside her. She had to get this over with, dissuade him from broaching the subject ever again. "She died from surgical complications just after I entered college. I have no one else."

He looked thoughtful. "And that must have factored in your decision to have Ryan after your engagement fell through, so you'd form your own family."

She let her silence convince him his deduction was right, when it was anything but.

"I'm very sorry to hear you were all alone in the world for so long. Coming from such an extensive family, I can't imagine how it must have been for you."

"I'm no longer alone."

"Yes." After a long moment when sympathy seemed to radiate off him, he smiled. "So we checked off passports, visas, fees and responsibility to family as reasons to resist my plans."

"But these are not the only…" She stopped, panting now as if she'd been trying to outrun an out-of-control car. She *was* trying to escape his inexorable intentions. "What am I saying? I'm not debating the feasibility of something that's not even an option. And the only thing that will make me feel better is that you drop this and…and…" She stopped again, feeling herself being backed into a trap her own capitulation would close shut. And he was standing there, waiting for her to succumb, knowing that she would. She groaned with helplessness, "Why even suggest this? Why not perform the surgery here? If it's because you're worried I'd be saddled with hospital expenses…"

He waved that majestic hand of his. "I could have had the hospital waive them by adding Ryan to the cases I was here for."

"Then why?" That came out a desperate moan.

He gave her such a look, that of someone willing to spend days cajoling and happy to do it. "You want reasons in descending or ascending order of importance?"

"Oh, please!" She tried to rise, failed to inject any co-ordination in her jellified legs. "Just...just..."

He sat down, put a soothing hand on her shoulder. "Breathe, Gwen. Everything will be fine, I promise. As for why, one main reason is that I can't stay away from my medical center any longer. And I certainly won't operate on Ryan, then leave him to someone else's follow-up. The other major reason is that I can only guarantee my results in a case as delicate when I'm in my medium, among the medical team I put together and the system I constructed."

Those *were* major reasons. "But still..."

"No 'but stills.' You're coming with me and..."

She interrupted him this time. "Even if we have to come, we don't have to right away. We can go back home, prepare ourselves, and when you have a surgery date arranged, we'd fly over."

He was the epitome of accommodation, yet of determination. "Why go to the trouble and expense when you have a free and convenient ride now? At absolutely no extra cost or effort on my part? And there's nothing to arrange. Once in Jizaan, I'll take Ryan for the mandatory pre-op tests, then do the surgery at once."

Her heart punched her ribs. "Th-that fast?"

"There's every reason to do it as soon as possible. But don't worry about a thing, I'll take care of everything."

"But I *can't* just let you do everything, pay for everything. If we have to go to Jizaan, then I'll at least pay our way."

He leaned back, folded his arms across his expansive chest. "So what do you propose to do? Give my pilot and cabin crew your credit card? Or will you want to stop by an ATM to get cash?"

"Please, don't joke! The most I can consent to not paying is your own fee. *If* you really waive it on a regular basis."

His face lost any lightness. "After all the things you implied I was, are you now calling me a liar?"

"Oh, God, *no!*" she blurted out. "I meant…"

His serious expression dissolved on a smile that could have powered a small city. She must be in even worse condition than she'd thought if she hadn't realized he *had* been joking.

"I know what you meant." His fingers gently probed her pulse. "Your heart is in hyperdrive. It's physically distressing thinking you'd be in someone's debt, isn't it?" *It's more your nearness, your touch,* she almost confessed. "But rest easy, Gwen, there's no debt. I will always owe many surgical successes to your expertise. Let me try to repay it with mine. As for me, on a professional level, adding the success of Ryan's surgery to my achievements will be more than payment enough for me." Suddenly the eyes that had become serious for real, crinkled on bedeviling. "But if you have money you can't bear having, I'll give you a list of causes in Jizaan and you can donate it in lieu of payment."

She had no answer now but more tears.

They welled up, filling her whole being. It was beyond incredible. To have his incomparable skills and support. It was also beyond terrible. To have to go with him, be near him, for weeks, be exposed to his influence and subjected to her weakness.

Beyond the tragedies that had sheared through her life and heart, that was the worst thing that could have happened to her. She would have gone to hell and wouldn't have bothered coming back to see Ryan healthy and happy. Now she would go to the one place she considered worse than hell. And she could never explain her feelings to Fareed.

She finally whispered, "I—I don't know what to say."

He sat back, his imposing frame sprawling in the contentment of someone who'd fulfilled his purpose. "You do. A three-letter word. Beginning with a *Y* and ending with an *S*."

A thousand fears screeched in the darkness of her mind. And she closed her eyes and prayed. That when she said it, it would only mean Ryan's salvation, and not her damnation.

She opened her eyes, stepped off the bleak, yet familiar, cliff of resignation into the abyss of the unknown.

And whispered the dreaded, "Yes."

The trip to Jizaan passed in a blur of distress.

Fareed, with Emad and the flight crew, orchestrated a symphony of such lavish luxury that it almost snapped her frayed nerves. She was so unused to being waited on, so uncomfortable at being on the receiving end of such indulgence, when she was unable to repay it, too, that it exhausted her.

After the first three hours, she'd escaped by sleeping the remaining eight hours to their refueling layover in London. She'd taken refuge in sleep again in the second leg of the journey, leaving Rose and Ryan to plumb the jet's inhabitants' ceaseless desire to spoil them.

She was floating somewhere gray and oppressive when she felt a caress on her hand.

She jerked out of the coma-like sleep knowing it was Fareed. Only his touch had ever felt like a thousand volts of disruption.

"I apologize for disturbing your slumber, but we're about to land." His eyes glowed like embers even in the jet's atrocious lighting, his magnificent voice soaked in gentle teasing. "I hope fourteen hours of sleep managed to provide a measure of rest."

She would have told him they sure hadn't if her throat didn't feel lined with sandpaper. She rose from the comfort of the plane bed, returning it to its upright position, feeling as if she'd been in a knock-down drag-out fight.

Apart from everything that disturbed her past, present and future, she knew why she felt wrecked. She might have been hiding in unawareness, but she'd felt him as she'd slept, and his thoughts, the demand, the promise in them and her struggle against them, had worn her out.

Rose waited until he left to approach her with Ryan, eyeing her in sarcastic censure. "That was sure record-breaking."

"You mean you and Ryan staying awake for that long?"

Rose huffed. "Oh, we slept, around an hour on each leg. *We* were savvy enough to take advantage of that once-in-a-lifetime experience. While *you* are either stupid, or stupid not to grab at all that…God offers."

From the proof of undeniable experience, Gwen knew that Rose, the only "aunt" she'd ever had, had only her best interest at heart. She'd always counted on her outspokenness to make her face the truth when she shied away from it. But now that smack of reality only made her sink deeper into despair.

Rose had no idea how…impossible everything was.

She was almost thankful when Fareed returned, bringing with him another dose of disturbance. She wasn't up to more evasive maneuvers with the other unstoppable force in her life.

She was unequivocally thankful when Rose engaged Fareed in conversation during landing. It left her able to pretend to look outside her window when she saw nothing but her internal turmoil.

They were really in Jizaan.

After touchdown, Fareed got up and took Ryan from Rose.

Gwen jumped up, tried to take him. Fareed looked down at Ryan. "Which ride do you want, *ya sugheeri?*"

Thorns sprouted in her stomach at the loving way Fareed called Ryan his little one.

Ryan, who seemingly understood anything Fareed said in either English or Arabic, looked back at her with dimples at full blast. Then he bobbed in his arms, spurring him to move.

There. She'd gotten her answer.

As Rose preceded them out of the plane with Emad, Fareed kept a step behind her.

His bass purr hit her back. "I'm not competing with you for his favor."

She slanted him a glance over her shoulder, almost winced at the incredible sight of him, as immaculate and fresh as if he hadn't been up for the past twenty-four hours, after a month of grueling surgeries, too. He towered over her, his shoulders broad enough to blot out the whole world, virility and gorgeousness radiating off him in shock waves.

Looking ahead before she stumbled, she murmured, "It never occurred to me that you were."

"And he's not choosing me over you."

A mocking huff broke from her. "Could have fooled me."

His deep chuckle resonated in her bones. "He's not. I'm just the new toy."

She would have chuckled, too, if she'd been able to draw more air than that which kept her on her feet and conscious.

And that was before he took her elbow, offered the support he must have felt she needed, smiled down at her. "You really should be happy we're enjoying each other's company so much." Her knees almost lost their solidity as seriousness tinged his gaze. "But I can't be more relieved that he likes and seeks me. The coming time isn't going to be easy, and trusting me is going to make everything so much better for him."

He was *that* thoughtful? She'd only ever known one other person with that kindness....

Memories lodged into her heart like an ax. She clamped down on the pain. She couldn't afford to let those overwhelm her now. She needed to be at her strongest, her most resolute. For Ryan. And for her own struggle.

She passed by a time zones clock, blinked at its verdict. Four-thirty in the afternoon in L.A., 5:30 a.m. in Jizaan. Exactly twenty-four hours from the moment she'd staggered into his orbit.

She felt as if her life before those hours had been someone else's, someone whose memories were sloughing off to be replaced by this new reality that had no rhyme or reason.

Then she stepped out of the jet and into another realm.

Her career had taken her all over the world, other desert kingdoms included, but Jizaan felt...alien, unprecedented.

The least of it was the airport itself, what she'd caught glimpses of from the air, what had the design, ambition and otherworldliness of a horizon-dominating space colony.

Everything else was painted with a brush of hyperreality. The star-sprinkled sky midway between the blue of eternity and the indigo of dawn had the vibrancy of another dimension, the stars the sharpness and abundance of another galaxy. The desert winter breeze that kissed her face and ran insistent fingers through her hair, even when jets' exhaust should have tainted it, felt cleansing, resuscitating. The whole atmosphere was permeated by echoes of a history rife with towering passions, unquenchable feuds and undying honor. She felt it all tug at her through her awareness of Fareed, whose blood ran thick with this land's legacy.

She stole a look at him, found him looking down at Ryan, his expression laced with fondness. Ryan, secure in Fareed's powerful grasp, was looking around, his face rapt as he inhaled deep, as if to breathe in the new place, make it a part of him.

Her heart constricted. If only…

"Ahlann wa sahlann bekom fi daari-wa daarakom."

Fareed's deep tones caressed every one of her nerves—until she translated what he'd said.

He was welcoming them to his home. And theirs.

She knew this was simply the ultragenerosity the region was known for, where they offered guests their homes as theirs. She still felt as if a wrecking ball had swung into her. She swayed with the force of the phantom sensation.

Fareed grabbed her tight against his side.

He'd probably saved her, this time from a plunge down a flight of steel stairs. But being ensconced in his heat and hardness, his concern was unendurable.

She groped for the railing, quickened her descent, pretending steadiness. The moment she touched ground, her legs wobbled again.

He caught her, exhaled. "I should have woken you earlier. You're still drowsy. Or you're hypoglycemic again. You barely ate anything since we started this journey."

She didn't refute his explanations. Better to let him think it was all physical. She wouldn't tell him the truth. She couldn't. Not the general truth. Or the one behind her latest bout of chaos. That as soon as her feet touched the ground, she could almost swear the land pulled at her. And yelled at her.

Leave, the moment you can. Before you sustain an injury you won't survive this time.

They'd reached the limo awaiting them a dozen feet from the jet's stairs, where Emad had taken the driver's seat with Rose beside him, when she heard Fareed say, "We're going to my place, Ryan."

The words meant for Ryan skimmed her mind, leaving no impression. Then they slowly sank. And detonated.

She swung to him as he held the door open for her. *"What?"*

He frowned his confusion. "What do you mean 'what'?"

"What do you mean *your* place?"

He smiled, a smile drenched in that overriding sensuality that was as integral to him as his DNA. "My place is the place where I live. And where you'll stay."

"We're going to stay in your center!"

He gave an adamant headshake as he prodded her to enter the limo, making her slide across the backseat by entering after her. "Only during the immediate pre- and postoperative period. And don't contest this again."

"I never contested it a first time...."

"Which was much appreciated, so don't suddenly change—"

She cut him off in return, feeling her brain overheating. "Because this is the first time I've heard of this."

"Not true. I told you during the flight."

"Was I awake when you told me?"

He gave her a thoughtful glance, then his smile scalded her with its amusement. "Come to think of it, that you didn't contest it should have clued me in that you were sleep talking."

"And now that I'm awake…"

"You'll be my esteemed guest."

Before she could utter another protest, Ryan, who'd been getting louder demanding his attention, grabbed his face and tugged. Fareed turned to him and at once they got engaged in another game of fetch-and-explain.

Even though he had been paying Ryan every attention, she knew he relished that timely excuse to end their conversation. She knew there was no use trying to continue it. He had this infallible way of getting his way, of making his unilateral decisions the only ones that made sense. But his place?

She felt she was sinking in quicksand and any move was making her sink faster.

And there was nothing she could do about it.

She exhaled, sought distraction, looked outside the window, her eyes finally registering the splendor of Jizaan's sparkling capital rushing by.

In the first slivers of dawn, the magnificence of Al Zaaferah, or The Victorious, named after the centuries-old ruling house, seeped into her awareness. It felt as if it had been erected today to the most lavish standards. It also looked constantly evolving with extreme-concept projects rising among the soaring mirrored buildings—

everything felt futuristic yet with pervasive cultural influences making it feel steeped in history.

She was lost in recording every detail when she noticed they'd gotten off the main roads and were now driving through automatic, thirty-feet-high, wrought-iron gates. Fareed's "place," no doubt.

The limo winded through ingeniously landscaped grounds, approaching a sprawling stone mansion crouching in the distance. Painted in sweeps of shadow and mysticism, it had the feel of a fortress from a Middle Eastern fable, the abode of someone who craved solitude, yet in having to house those his rank dictated, expanded his domain to give them space, and himself distance.

She hadn't thought what his place would be like. If she had, she would have imagined he lived in either the royal palace, or as imposing an edifice. But even though this place spoke of affluence, it didn't reek of excess. It was amazing how everything was permeated with the privileges of the prince, yet possessed the austerity of the surgeon.

All through their journey to the main door, she felt invisible eyes monitoring their progress, relaying it to forward stations. Even though she'd experienced many aspects of Fareed's status, that seamlessly orchestrated surveillance solidified everything in her mind. Who Fareed was. Where she was now.

He handed her out of the limo feet from stone steps leading to the patio. Footmen appeared as if from nowhere and rushed to open the massive brass-work doors.

She entered beside him with trepidation expanding in her heart into a columned hall that spread under a thirty-foot mosaic dome. The doors closed with a soft click. To Gwen, it felt as if iron prison doors were slammed shut behind her.

Her gaze darted around the indirectly lit space, got impressions of a sweeping floor plan extending on both sides, understated colors, a male influence in decor—his virile influence permeating the place. Her inspection ended where thirty-foot-wide stairs climbed to a spacious platform before winding away to each side of the upper floor.

Fareed led them up one side to a guest apartment triple the size of her condo, faithfully displaying the amalgam of modernity and Arabian Nights feel of the rest of the mansion. If she were in a condition to appreciate anything, she would have found it amazing to walk through doors that looked like they'd been transported through millennia intact only to swing open soundlessly with a proximity sensor. She was sure even Scheherazade's imagination couldn't have created anything like this place.

"Let me take him."

Gwen stirred from her reverie at Rose's words. She found her taking a now sound-asleep Ryan from Fareed.

"We're both done for." Rose stifled a yawn as she gave Gwen a kiss on the cheek. She grinned at Emad as she took Ryan's bag from him. "I'll find us the nearest beds and it might be night when you see either of us again."

In a minute everyone had left her alone with Fareed.

She turned blindly, pretending to inspect the sitting area. She ran a hand along the perfect smoothness of a hand-carved chair before turning to a spherical, fenestrated brass lantern hanging from the ceiling with spectacular chains. She made the mistake of transferring her gaze to him and the hypnotic play of light and shadows over his face and figure only deepened his influence.

He stared back at her for long, long moments, winding up the coil of tension inside her tighter until she felt she'd shatter.

Before she begged him to just stop, he finally exhaled.

"I apologize for not staying to show you around, but I have to go to work, catch up on everything I hadn't been able to attend to long-distance. Use the place as you would your own—and *don't* argue. Just explore, relax, rest. Then tomorrow we go the center."

Her heart almost knocked her off her feet. "You—you'll operate tomorrow?"

He simply said, "Yes."

After losing all of her family, one after the other, Gwen had thought she'd known all kinds of anguish and desperation. All forms of loss.

But now she knew there was more. There was worse. And there was one injury, one loss, she wouldn't survive.

If anything happened to Ryan...

"Everything will be fine."

She chafed at Rose's reassurance. What she'd reiterated over and over since Fareed had taken Ryan and disappeared into the depths of his staggeringly advanced medical center.

It didn't work now as it hadn't worked before. Fareed had come out once, fourteen hours ago, telling them Ryan had been prepared and was already in the O.R. He'd said he'd come out to reassure them as soon as he was done with the surgery.

That had lasted *eight* hours. Two hours longer than his longest estimate. Every second of the extra time, she'd known a worse hell than any she'd known before.

Guilt had consumed her. She'd sought inferior help initially, hoping it would suffice, save her from making contact with Fareed. What if she'd left it too late? What if she'd be punished for considering anything, no matter how momentous, ahead of Ryan's health?

Rose hugged her, sensing her thoughts. "Stop it, Gwen. Everything is fine. Fareed's assistant assured us it is."

"But *he* didn't."

Fareed hadn't come out to reassure her as he'd promised! What if that meant he couldn't face her with what had happened yet?

Rose tsked. "You did see the mass casualty situation that hit the center like a tornado, didn't you? With his being the chief around here and with God knows how many lives to save, I'm sure putting your mind to rest personally plunged to the bottom of his priorities."

Logic droned that Rose was right. But hysteria was drowning it out. They wouldn't let her see Ryan in Recovery or ICU. Fareed's orders. That was six mutilating hours ago.

Suddenly, Fareed appeared at the other end of the expansive waiting area.

She rose, could barely stand erect as his long strides ate the maddening distance between them. Then out of the blue, he was swamped by people. Other patients' frantic families.

He stopped his advance, turned to them with calm, patient and what must have been very detailed reassurance because it defused their tension. By the time he at last excused himself with utmost courteousness and resumed his path to her, she was at screaming pitch.

As he stopped before her, those fiery eyes piercing her, she felt he'd trodden on the heart that had crashed at his feet.

"It all went wrong."

Six

Gwen's lifeless statement barely scratched the surface of the terror in her heart.

Fareed hadn't smiled at her. He'd smiled at the others. She could only interpret his intensity as bad news. The worst...

He smiled. Her knees buckled.

"*Nothing* went wrong." His smile broadened as he caught her by the waist, stopped her from folding to the ground. "I *already* told you that—well, I sent Akram to tell you that everything went perfectly right."

"Oh, you magnificent man, thank you!" Rose charged him, made him relinquish his hold on Gwen and squeezed him in an exuberant hug.

Gwen felt the life force that had felt extracted from her slowly begin to reenter her body. Then he put Rose at arm's length, smiled down at her. "But I can't take much credit. Ryan did most of the work. From the pre-op preps to what my team told me felt like ordering his very tissues to assist me, he was the most interactive patient I ever had. I've never had a surgery go so smoothly."

Rose laughed her delight. "That's our Ryan! But we'll just pretend that you did have an equal role in this, and you'll accept our thanks like a good sport."

"As long as you realize the extent of my contribution, I'm happy to accept."

Their elation hammered at Gwen, demanding to breach her numbness. But the tidal wave hovered at the periphery of her mind, scared to crash and sweep her fears away.

"So why won't you let me see him?"

He turned to her, eyes flaring with sympathy. "Because children look heartrending when they're in ICU and I wanted to spare you the sight."

"*That* was why you left me to go insane out here for six hours? Didn't you realize I'd prefer having my heart rent by seeing him over going mad by not seeing him?"

His eyes widened with her every word, before they narrowed again with self-derision. "My concern was evidently misplaced. Guess I can't put myself in a mother's shoes after all."

Her frustration turned inward, a flame that burned her blood with mortification. "God, no...I didn't mean to imply that..."

"Don't apologize for loving Ryan too much. But even after you blasted me for being so blithely insensitive to your needs, I am still unable to meet them. I have to be this infuriating professional and insist on my position. For now. I promise you he's in perfect condition and that you'll see him in a few hours."

"Please, let me see him now. A look is all I want!"

"What you *don't* want is the image of him sedated and inert and hooked to tubes and monitors burned into your memory. You may know what you'll see, but seeing it for real is something totally different. And I refuse to let you inflict another mental scar on yourself. I've seen parents suffer debilitating anxiety long after their children are cured, and you've suffered enough of that. So even though you probably want to kill me right now, you might want to thank me later."

"But I don't want…" She paused, groaned. "Are—are you doing this on purpose?"

He chuckled, winked at Rose who joined him in chuckling. "Of course, I am. One of my PhDs is in distraction. But while it must feel like eternity now, the hours will pass, then I'll transfer him to a private suite and you'll be with him from then on." His logic was putting out the fires of dread and desperation. But the clamoring of her heart wouldn't subside. He silenced her turmoil. "Until then, how about you ladies join me for a meal? I've long passed starving, and knowing you, Gwen, I'm sure we were on that same path together."

Rose waved her hand. "Oh, you two go ahead. Emad told me to call him as soon as you made an appearance, and to meet him in the center's restaurant. He promised a meal to top the Cordon Bleu he treated me to in L.A., and I sure want to see how this can be achieved." Rose hugged her. "See? You should always listen to me. Now listen to me and take care of yourself. You won't do Ryan any good if you collapse. You're even allowed to smile without sinning against motherhood."

"I'll take care of her." Fareed took Gwen's elbow. "I'll even brave the impossible chore of making her smile." He tilted his head at her from his prodigious height. "Shall we?"

Gwen didn't even nod. She could do nothing but stare

after Rose, as she walked away with her phone at her ear, and let Fareed steer her wherever he wished.

She registered glimpses of their journey down the halls and corridors spread in reflective granite. She barely noticed the people whose eyes held deference for Fareed and curiosity for her on their way to an elevator straight out of a sci-fi movie. She didn't feel it move, but when its brushed-steel doors slid open moments later, it was into a room the size of a tennis court, with twenty-foot, floor-to-ceiling windows spanning its arched side.

It was like looking out of a plane, with Al Zaaferah and its skyscrapers sprawling below and into the horizon, lighting up the clear night sky like a network of blazing jewels. She dimly realized they must be in the top floors of the steel-and-glass tower that formed the main portion of the center.

She'd barely recovered from the breathtaking elevation when the opulence and austerity of the place hit her. This must be his office.

His hand burned its mark into her arm as he escorted her across a gleaming hardwood floor covered in what felt like acres of Persian silk carpet to a deepest-green leather couch ensemble around a unique worked-wood centerpiece table.

When she remained standing, he gave her the gentlest of tugs. She collapsed where he indicated. He stood before her for a long moment, his gaze storming through her. Then his lips spread.

Her heart tried its best to leap out of her throat.

"Even though I know asking your preference in food is an exercise of futility, it seems I like butting my head against a wall. So, again, any favorite cuisine?"

"Anything…with calories."

She was stunned she'd produced the words. She was only sure she had when he laughed.

Her hand pressed the painful, thudding lump that had replaced her heart. There should be a law against such hazardous behavior.

He phoned in his order of food before he turned his attention back to her. Beside that watchfulness that made her feel he was listening to her thoughts, and that supreme assurance that was integral to him, she saw satisfaction.

From what she knew of him from years of following his career, this was a man who knew his handiwork, never exaggerated his results. He really believed Ryan's surgery had been successful beyond even what he'd promised her.

And the floodgates of relief finally burst.

She shook under its enormity, and this time when he reached for her, she surrendered to the potent comfort he offered.

Fareed stroked Gwen's shining head, absorbed her softness and ebbing fear, inhaled her freshness and dissipating distress and told his burning hands that that was as far as it went—for now.

When he'd come out of the O.R., he'd seen no one but her. She'd looked so lost, those eyes that wreaked havoc with his control pleading for reassurance. He'd forced himself to answer the other families first or he would have crushed her in his arms. As it were, he'd been aware of the curious glances when he'd taken her to his private elevator.

Not that he cared. He did his absolute best for all his patients. If he chose to give his personal time and attention afterward to her, it was no one's business.

But holding her like that, having her burrow into him like a kitten seeking protection, was wrecking his reason.

His body had hardened beyond arousal, and that was with her wrapped in those shapeless clothes and only seeking comfort. What effect would she have if she sought him with hunger in her touch and eyes?

He shuddered with expectation. What he'd give to carry her to bed *now* and to hell with his professional code.

But he'd already strained that code for her. All he could do now was keep his passion under a tight leash until Ryan was no longer in his care. Afterward...

Afterward, he expected an even fiercer impediment than the dictates of his professional honor. His father.

He knew he'd wage a more ferocious war with him than when he'd chosen to go into medicine and not into politics or business.

Not that it mattered. He wasn't Hesham, young and vulnerable. He would fight anything and anyone, starting with his father, to have her. He'd face the whole world for her.

And he knew that, beyond a doubt, she wanted him as fiercely. That was what fueled her struggle to keep her distance, what she believed the circumstances dictated. But when her worry for her son and his obligations ended, he would plumb the depth of her answering need.

Feeling he was peeling off a layer of skin, he let her go as soon as her tremors subsided. She pulled away at the same instant.

Embarrassment blazed on her cheeks as she slid to the end of the couch. "You must be so sick of soothing frantic relatives."

"It's part of the job description."

He nearly laughed at his exaggeration. She'd seen how he'd dealt with his patients' relatives. While he'd been courteous and accommodating, he hadn't dissolved their fears in his embrace.

A knock on the door roused him. "Our calories are here." A smile wobbled on her lips. He sighed. "Next time, I'll manage to make that smile last longer than a nanosecond."

He went to the door, returned with a trolley laden with food and beverages. Everything smelled mouth-watering. But the hunger that rose inside him was for her. He could almost taste the grace and femininity in her every line. His body tightened even more.

He should be exhausted. He was. It made no difference when she was around. He remained alert, unable to waste one moment when he could...experience her. Even when she'd slept on the plane, he'd stayed awake to check on her. She aroused not only his passion but his protectiveness, too, to unreasoning levels.

Bowled over. That was what he was. And to think that before he'd seen her, he'd sighed in pity at those who used that expression. Reveling in his condition, he sat down beside her, started uncovering hot plates.

He whistled. "Seems they got us *everything* with calories. Are you up to the challenge?"

Fareed's question distracted her from drooling at the distressing scent. Not the food's. His.

She could only murmur, "No promises."

His fire-tinged eyes turned more enigmatic before he turned to serve the food. Her senses reeled with his closeness, her thoughts tangling at his inconsistencies.

Even though he was known to be most accessible professionally, on a personal level, he was considered inapproachable. Yet from her own experience, he was only too approachable, and she...

She *had* to stop fantasizing about him. He was the one

man she should never want, the one man who was off-limits.

But what if he is the one man you can *want?*

She crushed the insidious voice as she accepted a steaming plate piled with mouth-watering grilled salmon and vegetables, careful not to touch him again. Touching him had infused a dangerous narcotic into her bloodstream. She should be careful not to end up addicted. Or was she already?

Was this how it happened? Inadvertent exposure, moments of surrender to temptation and suddenly you were irrevocably lost....

"Eat, Gwen, and I'll reward you. I'll discuss Ryan's postoperative period and rehabilitation."

This brought her back to earth with a thud.

"Yes, please."

His eyes ignited. She shied away from their heat and her interpretation of it. It had to be her feverish mind superimposing her preposterous cravings on his glances and actions.

She cleared her throat. "Wh-what do you expect?"

"How about a deal?" he countered. "One mouthful a sentence."

"Oh, all right." She loaded a fork, forced it into her mouth.

He tutted. "A bigger mouthful won't get you a longer sentence, and I won't talk any faster if you choke."

She swallowed the lump and almost did just that.

"For God's sake, just tell me!" she spluttered.

"I expect a full recovery." At her evident frustration with his brevity, his eyebrows rose. "You expected more for that forkful? I already had Akram tell you everything. You just want me to repeat myself to see if I'll slip up."

Heat surged to her head. "I realize I'm being obsessive…"

"And I'm totally ribbing you, as you say in the States." His eyes laughed at her, coaxing her to ease up. "But as a scientist, too, I realize you won't be satisfied until you have all the details. So let's start with my findings during surgery."

Her heart jumped. He understood. That she needed to know what he'd seen with his own eyes, fixed with his own hands. That only specifics would make it all real.

"The defect was long and the tethering was more than I'd hoped. The meninges were also prolapsed. But I corrected it all with a procedure I have been developing. It takes double the time of any other procedure—yes, that's why I took longer than projected—but it ensures no scarring and no future retethering. The nerve roots were minimally damaged, but with Ryan's fast growth, and the sites of the tethering, progressive damage would have occurred within the next months. So your persistence couldn't have been more warranted, and the timing of the surgery couldn't have proved more critical. Now, with physiotherapy and a four-month course of your drug, Ryan should regain his legs' full power and sensation, and I don't expect there to be any problems with toilet training."

Tears welled up again as the certainty she'd needed seeped into her bones. "I—I can't find words to thank you."

He grimaced. "Then don't go in search of any." He tapped her plate with his fork. "Now eat. You need to be stocked up on as many calories as you can to be there for Ryan in the coming time."

She ended up finishing a three-course meal.

But taking a leaf from his repertoire, she specified

a reward in return. Letting her see Ryan as soon as she was done.

He'd finally succumbed, telling her she drove a hard bargain.

She'd been standing for what felt like hours behind the glass partition in pediatric ICU, gowned for the sterile zone, watching Ryan sleeping in a cot that looked like a space pod, her tears streaming. Ones of pure relief.

Even though it drove a hot lance through her heart to see Ryan's little body hooked to leads and invaded by drips and tubes, she knew one thing beyond a doubt: he was all right.

Fareed had been sharing the poignant vigil in silence.

He finally inhaled. "And Ryan invalidates my worries again. He looks as if he's sleeping in complete contentment."

"H-he probably is," she whispered. "He must feel how much care he's receiving, must have felt how much you've done for him. He might be relieved for the first time in his life now you've corrected h-his problem."

"Everything's possible, especially with a child as sensitive as Ryan." He turned her to him, wiped a tear that was trembling on her chin. "Now go say welcome back to your baby."

She gasped. "Oh, God...really?"

He nodded, his smile a ray of delight illuminating her world.

She streaked into the ICU. He followed at a slower pace.

He stood back patiently, let her fondle and coo to the sedated Ryan until she turned to him with tears mixing with unbridled smiles. Then he checked Ryan, discussed his management with his ICU staff, before escorting her out.

He took her to a suite on the same level as his office.

The sitting room overlooked the same view that had stunned her from his windows, from a different viewpoint, with the magic of the capital now shrouded in another dawn. She could barely believe it had been just a day since she'd set foot in Jizaan.

He took her by the shoulders. "I recommend another fourteen-hour sleep marathon. Or at least eight. Don't wake up sooner on Ryan's account. I'm keeping him in ICU for twelve more hours."

"But you said you'd let him out in a few hours!"

"And the concrete numerical value of 'a few' is?"

He was teasing her again. But now she knew in her bones Ryan would be all right, she found herself attempting to tease back.

"The world doesn't know how lucky it is that you decided to use your inexorableness for good. But even though you've benevolently steam-rolled me on every decision and I'm now forever in your debt, this—" her gesture encompassed the superbly decorated, all-amenities, expansive suite "—is going too far. Between here and the guest apartment at your place, you'll spoil Ryan and Rose so much that I might have to find us a new place when we return home."

Interest flared in his eyes. "Where *is* home? We never got around to talking about that."

She almost kicked herself. She'd just given him an opening to delve deeper into her life and everything she wanted kept hidden at all costs.

Panic surged. If she told the truth, he'd put things together sooner rather than later. If she lied, rather than omitted the truth, as she had done so far, apart from when she'd had to lie about Ryan's father, those same powers of observation would see through her. But she had no choice.

A lie was potentially less catastrophic than the truth.

Feeling it would corrode her on the way out, she opened her mouth to deliver it…and his pager went off.

She almost sagged when he released her from his focus.

Then her breath caught. He was frowning at his pager. "Is it Ryan?"

He raised his eyes at her question, gave a lock of her hair a playful tug. "*No*, Gwen. Ryan is fine and will remain fine. It's just another emergency. Now have mercy on me and sleep. I'm exhausted already and it'll be a while before I get any rest. Don't add to my burdens. I'll *know* if you're not sleeping."

Without waiting for an answer, he turned away.

The door closed behind him in seconds. But she still felt his presence surrounding her, making her world secure, and life no longer a setting for anguish and struggles.

She could offer him nothing in return for the gifts he'd showered on her and her own. A chunk of her life wouldn't suffice. But he'd asked her to make his easier by taking herself off his endless list of worries. Complying with his request was all she had to offer for now.

She found the bedroom, and with a moan, sank into the bed's luxury, into the depths of thankfulness. For him, for Ryan's cure. And for being saved by the pager.

She prayed she'd never be forced to lie to him outright again, until he discharged Ryan.

Once he did, she'd run, disappear, and he'd never know.

And she'd never see him again.

The joy that had begun to take root inside her drained. Tears flowed again as she prayed.

Let his obligations keep him away for as long as she had to remain in Jizaan. Let his loss start now.

Only that would save her from sustaining further injuries.

Seven

She should have known.

That anything she hoped for would happen in reverse. With the record of the past years, how had she hoped otherwise?

Apart from Ryan's healing at a breathtaking rate, blossoming under Fareed's comprehensive care, everything else was going wrong. Terribly wrong.

For the week they stayed in the center, Fareed was constantly present. She knew this wasn't true, that he disappeared for hours but he came back so often, in her amplified awareness of him, it felt like he was always there, giving her no respite.

After dreading being in his place, where everything echoed with his feel and was soaked in his presence, she couldn't wait to go back there. She hoped that with him at work during the day, and hopefully returning home exhausted, she'd see less of him. But for the following four weeks, the opposite again happened. He came home too often, too unpredictably, so she couldn't brace for his appearance, worsening her condition at every exposure.

Everyone in the center had told her he made them feel he *was* omnipresent. She could well believe it. After the endless hours in the O.R., consultations, follow-ups and administrative chores, not to mention his duties as a prince, which he said he'd lately limited to steering the kingdom's health system, as if that wasn't huge enough, she couldn't figure out how he had time for her. Not to mention had a life. A private life…

Her throat tightened as it did each time that thought forced its reality on her. It was ridiculous to feel that way, but still…contemplating the horde of glamorous women who no doubt pursued him, of whom he took the most voluptuous and beautiful to bed…

Peals of laughter, masculine and childish, wrenched her mind away from the images, only for different ones to superimpose themselves. The images that would be engraved in her mind, seared into her soul forever. The sight of Fareed and Ryan together, bonding, reveling in each other.

But as painful as the sight was, it was also incredible. And worth any future suffering to live through.

Fareed was sitting with Ryan on the floor, in the middle of his mansion's family room, wrapped up in their game, caressed by the warm, golden lights of polished brass sconces that illuminated the expansive space. The French doors leading to the massive terrace were wide open and the gauzy cream curtains were billowing in the desert's cool evening breeze. The unpolished sand-colored marble floor was spread in hand-woven kilims and scattered in huge cushions covered with the same designs and vivid hues. Fareed had said those were the Aal Zaafers' tribal patterns and colors, intricate combinations of stripes and rhomboids, in vibrant crimsons, gold and greens. He'd also said the room had never been used. Until them.

As if she needed more heartache, to know he'd been welcoming them in the place reserved for his future family.

Before they'd settled down for the evening here, they'd finished another physiotherapy session with Ryan. He'd turned another of the mansion's rooms into a rehabilitation center, and had turned those uncomfortable, exhausting and sometimes painful sessions into Ryan's most antici-pated playtime.

Now he was playing catch with Ryan. After giving Ryan easy catches to get him excited and motivated, he'd throw one out of reach and have him eagerly crawling to fetch.

He was always thinking of another exercise for Ryan, another method to gauge his improvement. He'd made an art of helping Ryan enjoy it, participate wholeheartedly, and subsequently heal faster, develop more power and better coordination.

He now threw the soft red ball on the huge square table that paralleled the couch she sat on. Ryan hurtled after it, reached the table, then stopped, an absorbed expression painting his face as he contemplated his dilemma.

She transferred her gaze to Fareed. "Seems you've given him a challenge he's not up to...yet."

Fareed shrugged, his face spread in the warmth that messed her up inside. "He hasn't given up yet. Let's see what he'll do."

She nodded even as her heart constricted. Every cell in her longed to end Ryan's frustration, give him the ball. But Fareed had been teaching her not to coddle him, to drive him to achieve his potential, and be as loving or even more so while at it.

Ryan finally approached one of the table's corners. Then after some internal debate, pulled himself up in degrees until he unfolded to his feet, stood braced at its edge. Her heart boomed.

It was the first time he'd ever stood up!

Her eyes flew to Fareed. He looked as moved, his smile as proud as hers. But when she moved to get the ball for Ryan, he gave her an imperative "wait" gesture.

She waited. And under her disbelieving, delighted eyes, Ryan hooked his right leg, the one that had always been weaker, over the edge of the table and pulled himself on top of it.

Once there, he weaved through worked-silver plates, gleaming copper candleholders and glass planters like a cat, knocking nothing over. Once he reached his quarry, he grabbed it, waved it at her in delighted victory.

"You did it, darling," she said, forcing back tears, her smile so wide that it hurt. "You got the ball because you're brilliant and strong and determined and the most wonderful boy on earth."

After a satisfactory dose of adulation, he remembered his playmate, the one he wanted to impress most.

Ryan reversed his way across the table, backed off its edge carefully. Once his feet touched ground, he plopped back down, catching his breath after the unprecedented endeavor.

Then he turned to Fareed, shrieking his triumph and throwing his trophy back to him.

He caught it, stuffed it beneath his arm and treated Ryan to a boisterous round of applause. Ryan zoomed to him, sought the haven of his arms. After having enough of

Fareed's validation, Ryan wriggled off and crawled away as if eager to resume their game.

Before following, Fareed spared her a glance, eyes twinkling with pride. "See? Nothing is beyond him. He's creative and problem-solving and ambitious and he'll always surpass your expectations."

She barely stifled the cry. *Stop surpassing mine! Stop making me want you more when I can't even dream of you.*

But it was already too late.

She'd come to depend on him when it was the worst thing she could have done. She couldn't think of a time when he wouldn't be in her life, their lives, when it was inevitable.

She'd fallen in love with him when it would mean destruction.

Yes, she loved him.

And she would have preferred it if he didn't realize she was alive. But she could no longer escape what she'd known from the moment he'd captured her gaze at that conference. He'd made it clear, in a hundred nuances, what he wanted from her, that he was only waiting until any doctor/patient's parent trace of their relationship had faded, to act on his desire.

His desire to have her in his bed.

And even though guilt and dread haunted her, this was the only place she wanted to be.

But it didn't matter what she wanted. She couldn't act on her desire. She wouldn't.

"I'm surprised he hasn't melted yet."

Rose. Sitting right beside her and she hadn't even noticed her come in.

Rose elaborated, "I've seen hunger blazing in eyes before, but the solar flares in yours...yowza!"

Her gaze moved nervously to Fareed, who was far

enough away not to catch Rose's comments. Thank goodness. If Rose had seen it, had he…?

Who was she kidding? He had. He knew he had her on the brink of mindlessness. And he'd been letting her know, subtly, inexorably, how he'd leave her no place to run when he made his move, how earth-shattering it would be when he claimed her.

She let out a resigned exhalation. "Don't start, Rose."

Rose repaid her with a fed up look. "Then why don't *you* stop? Jumping away as if he scalds you each time he comes near?"

"What do you expect? The man has a magnetic field that could upset a planet's orbit." After a moment's hesitation, she admitted, "He does scald me."

Rose nudged her. "Then help yourself to his inferno, girl."

She squeezed her eyes. "I can't, and you know it."

"So you've been mourning. Now enough." Rose turned fully to her, scowling. "Let the dead rest and get on with your life."

Gwen bit her lip, memories a shard embedded in her heart. "It's not only mourning."

"What else is it? Can't be Ryan because Fareed is the best thing that has ever happened to him, present company included."

"You're talking as if Fareed is in Ryan's life in anything more than a temporary way, when you know he's just his surgeon…."

"He's not just his surgeon, and *you* know it."

For a heart-wrenching moment, Gwen thought Rose knew. Who Fareed really was to Ryan.

But there was no way that she did. She hadn't been in her life for the past five years, had missed all the developments and upheavals that had ripped through her life.

Rose knew only what she'd told her once everything had been over. She didn't know about Ryan's parentage. And she must never know.

Rose turned her eyes to the man and baby who possessed Gwen's heart. "I mean…just look at them." Gwen didn't *want* to look. It hurt too much. "Look at *you*. You're burning for him." Gwen averted her eyes, damned being so transparent. "Then look at *him*. He would devour you whole if you didn't flit around like a hummingbird on speed."

A chuckle burst out of Gwen. Only Rose could cut to the truth, yet make it somehow bearable, even light-hearted. "And you recognize the symptoms because you and Emad are suffering from the same condition?"

Rose wouldn't be distracted. "Emad and I have *nothing* like the same condition. *I* don't have melodramatic tendencies and I'm not letting self-perpetuated worries stop me from taking whatever happiness I can now. We're free grown-ups with nothing to stop us from having whatever we want together. Apart from your baffling reluctance, I can say the same about you and Fareed."

Gwen exhaled dejectedly. "I'm not free."

"Because you're a single mother? And I can't fathom your position because I'm not? So enlighten me, what are women in your situation supposed to do? Sacrifice your personal lives at the altar of your children's upbringing?"

Gwen stared sightlessly at the mansion's gardens. She wished with all her heart that she could share her burden with Rose, that everything wasn't so complicated, so impossible.

Why had Fareed of all men turned out to be the one who awakened the woman in her? And so completely, so violently?

To add to her heartache, Rose added, "And anyway,

don't knock temporary. You of all people know that nothing, starting with life itself, is permanent. Think about that and make up your mind."

She swallowed a lump at another impending and permanent loss. "My mind is made up, Rose."

Before Rose could counterattack, Fareed's rich baritone curled around Gwen's sensitized nerves, filling her with regret for what would never be.

He was walking toward them, with Ryan in his arms. He'd said, "I have an announcement to make."

Her heart pounded so fast that she felt the beats merging like the wings of the hummingbird Rose had compared her to.

Fareed stopped before them, so beautiful and vital that a fist of longing squeezed her heart, stilled it into its grip.

"I've done and redone every test there is. And the verdict is in. This magnificent boy is on his way to a full recovery. I expect he'll walk in a few months' time."

Gwen's hands shot to her lips, stifled her soundless cry.

She'd been monitoring Ryan's every notch of improvement obsessively, and from her experience with neurological progress, she'd been hoping for the best. But to have Fareed spell out such concrete conviction, put a time frame on it, made it all real.

Ryan *would* walk!

She raced with Rose to Fareed to drown him in thanks, to pluck Ryan from his arms, then from each other's to deluge him in kisses. Ryan thought this was a new game and threw himself from one set of arms to another, giggling his delight.

But as Emad joined them and dinner followed, Gwen's euphoria drained gradually.

She'd known the day when Fareed would announce the completion of his role in Ryan's care was fast-approaching.

She couldn't have hoped for a better outcome. There *was* no better outcome. For Ryan.

For her...

It was clear from everything Fareed said and did that he thought this day would mark the beginning of that temporary inferno Rose had urged her to hurtle into. *She* knew it would only herald the end. She'd thought she'd be ready for it. She wasn't.

As their "family" evening continued, Fareed's nearness only made it harder. She couldn't stop herself from feasting on his presence like it was her last meal.

And he made it worse still by no longer tempering the desire in his eyes, by barely touching his food, too, showing her that the only thing he hungered for was her.

For the rest of the evening, as she escaped his unspoken intentions, she struggled to convince herself that walking away would be survivable.

Gwen was suffocating.

Tentacles were tightening around her throat, cutting off air and blood, holding her back. Her arms reached out, but the tentacles jerked her tighter, immobilized her. The shadow she was reaching for tumbled in macabre slow-motion down the abyss....

"No!"

She heard the shout ring out even as she felt it tear out of her depths...and her eyes shot open.

She jerked up, her hands tearing at the nonexistent noose.

It had been another nightmare.

Knowing that didn't help. She still gasped, trembled, feeling like the day of the accident all over again. Crushed, torn, strangled by panic and helplessness.

In the months since, night terrors had plagued whatever

sleep she'd succumbed to. During the day, anxiety attacks had dismantled her psyche. It hadn't helped that she knew there had been nothing she could have done.

She stumbled out of the bed. It was 2:00 a.m. She'd barely slept an hour. No use thinking she'd sleep again tonight. She was afraid to, anyway.

She went to Ryan's room, checked on him even though she'd heard his steady breathing over the baby monitor. She found him on his back, which he hadn't done since the surgery, his arms flung over his head in abandon. She kissed him and he murmured something satisfied, melting her heart with thankfulness.

She went downstairs, roamed the seemingly deserted mansion, her steps as restless as her mind.

She felt Fareed all over, his scent clinging to her lungs, caressing her senses. And it wasn't because this was his domain. She'd feel him across the world. And she would, for the rest of her life.

And now, it was over. There was no more reason to stay here. She'd take her tiny family and leave Jizaan in the morning.

And he'd never know how she really felt. But that mattered nothing. What mattered was that he never knew who she really was....

"Do you know what you are?"

Fareed's hypnotic tones hit her with the force of a quake.

She jerked around, her gaze slamming to the top of the stairs, the side leading to his quarters.

He wasn't there. Had she imagined hearing him? Were her dread and guilt playing tricks on her?

Then his voice hit her again. "What I thought when I first saw you? A magical being from another realm."

She almost sagged. He was here. And he hadn't meant what she'd feared.

"And do you have any idea about the extent of my craving for you? How long it has gone unfulfilled? How much it has cost me to suppress it, to stay away from you?"

Each beat of her heart rocked her as a shadow detached itself from the depth of darkness engulfing the upper floor, taking his form. His body solidified, his influence intensified with every step. Then his face emerged from the shadows and she gasped.

Even from this distance, there was no mistake.

The ultra-efficient surgeon, the indulgent benefactor, the teasing, patient playmate was gone. A man of tempestuous passion had emerged in his place.

Making it worse was seeing him for the first time in what he'd been born to wear, an *abaya* that looked tailored of Jizaan's moonless skies themselves.

And she had no right to his passion. She'd lose even the bittersweet torment of his nearness tomorrow. She'd never again feel as alive.

"You sensed me." His voice reverberated inside her as he descended the stairs. "You knew I was coming to you, came to meet me halfway. You knew that I would no longer wait."

Something snapped inside her. Her paralysis shattered.

She needed to tell him…something, anything of the truth, if only that of her feelings, her needs. To have something, anything of him. Just this once.

He quickened his descent as she moved toward him, the *abaya* billowing around him like a shroud of darkest magic. Her feet felt as if they were gaining momentum from his power, his purpose, that force that had entered her life to change the face of her world forever.

Then he stopped. At the platform where the stairs diverged, as if giving her a last chance to retreat.

She stopped, too, three steps beneath him, momentum lost, confessions fled. She looked up at him, overwhelmed. He was even more than she'd ever dreamed.

The obsidian silk *abaya* draped over his endless shoulders, pleated for miles to his bare feet, falling open over the perfection of his chiseled, raven hair-dusted chest and abdomen. The low-riding drawstring pants of the same color and material hugged his thighs, hiding none of the power of his muscles, or that of his arousal.

He seemed as if he'd stepped out from another time, a force of nature and of the supernatural, poured into solid form. But it was the fever radiating from him, the same one that raged through her, that shook her most—setting free the one confession she could make.

"I don't want you to wait."

Eight

Something unbridled flared in Fareed's eyes.

Gwen's breathing stopped. She stood mesmerized by the ferocity that ate her up, finished her. Now...now he'd descend the last steps separating them, sweep her up in his arms....

But what he did stopped her heart. With shock.

She would have never expected that he would...*laugh*.

But he did. Peal after peal of pure male amusement.

His laughter mortified her even as it inflamed her.

What had she said or done that he found so funny?

Maybe it was her braid, mommy robe and fluffy slippers? And the cartoon character pajamas beneath?

God, *of course* it was. He must have gotten a good look at her and rethought his intentions. No wonder he was laughing.

All thoughts scattered as he moved, still laughing, until he was on the same step, bearing down on her with his heat and virility. Then he leaned down, put his lips to her ear.

"I just have one question—" each syllable, each feathering of his lips shot arousal right to her core "—will you ever stop surprising me?"

She raised confused eyes up to his, found fire simmering just below the mirth.

"You exhausted me at every turn," he whispered, intimate, maddening, "contesting my every declaration, my every decision, the minor before the major. Then I tell you I'm taking you to my bed and you just…agree?"

Her gaze wavered as his eyes lost their lightness, flames rising higher. She shivered as her own fever spiked in answer.

Then to her amazement, she heard her voice, husky with hunger and provocation. "I didn't exactly say I agree."

He caught her around the waist, slammed her against his hard length. Her breath and heartbeats emptied against his chest.

Twisting her braid around his wrist, harnessing her by it, ferocity barely leashed with gentleness, he tilted up her face, his eyes now a predator's excited by his mate's unexpected challenge.

His next words poured almost in her gasping mouth. "You said better. You commanded me not to wait. Now I'll obey you, *ya fatenati*. No more waiting, ever again."

Then he bent and swept her feet from beneath her, cut her every tie to gravity and sanity.

She went limp in his hold, becoming weightless, timeless, directionless, as she lay ensconced in his arms. She burrowed into him as the world moved in hard, hurried thuds, each one hitting her with vertigo, the pressure of emotion almost snuffing out her consciousness, like that day lifetimes ago.

And that was before he pressed his lips to her forehead

in a branding kiss. "Never stop surprising me, *ya sahe-rati.*"

She almost blurted out that *he* was the enchanter, the sorcerer. She choked on the words. She hadn't let on that she knew Arabic, couldn't bear lying if he asked why she did.

Every anxiety vanished as he relinquished his hold on her and she sank in the depths of soft dark beddings, was shrouded by the golden warmth of gaslight and the intoxication of incense and craving.

Then he came down over her.

She moaned with the blast of stimulation, emotional and sensual, of her first exposure to the reality of him, his weight and bulk and hunger, the physicality of his passion.

He rose off her, slid her robe off. She felt a blush creeping up from her toes to her hairline as he exposed her pajamas.

"Bugs Bunny." He shook his head in disbelief. "And if I find you arousing beyond endurance in this, I might not survive seeing you in something made to worship your beauty."

She crossed her hands over her chest, burning with self-consciousness. "I know how I look in this thing. I picked it to match one of Ryan's…"

"Answer me this other question, Gwen." His hand unlocked hers, before imprisoning them over her head in one of his. "Will I always have to say something over and over before you consider believing me? Will you ever believe I only ever say what I mean?"

She felt her flush deepening. "It's not you I'm doubting."

"Then how can you doubt your own beauty, your effect on me? If anything, I'm holding back, not telling you what you really make me feel, what I really want to do to you."

His eyes flared with mock-threat and too-real lust. "I don't want to scare you."

She shook her head against the sheets. "You won't ever scare me. Show me everything you feel."

Her ragged words elicited a smile that was sheer male triumph and assurance. "*Amrek, ya rohi*—command me."

Yet his hands trembled in her hair as they undid her braid, spread its thickness around her. Then he buried his face in it, breathed her in hard, let her hear in his ragged groans that he was at the mercy of his need for her as she was for him.

"I've wanted you, I've needed this…" He bore down on her harder, pressed all of him into all of her. "Your flesh and desire, you scent and feel, since the first moment I saw you all those years ago. I craved you until I was hollow. Now you're here and you'll be mine, at last, Gwen…*at last*."

She whimpered her agreement, her eagerness. He swooped up to capture the sound, his lips taking hers in a hot, moist seal, enveloping, dissolving, his tongue thrusting into her recesses, in total tasting, in thorough possession.

She'd imagined this until she'd felt *she'd* be forever empty, too, if she never experienced it. But this far surpassed the imaginings that had tormented her. The power and profundity of his kiss, his feel and scent, and his taste…his *taste*…

He bit into her lower lip, stilled its tremors in a nip so leashed, so carnal that it had her opening wider, deepening his invasion.

Just as she felt she'd come apart, he severed their meld, groaned, "Gwen, *habibati, hayaati, abghaaki, ahtaajek*."

She sobbed again as she pulled him back. He'd called her his love, his life, said he coveted her, *needed* her.

She knew those were the exaggerated endearments his culture indulged in. They didn't have to be literally meant, and in those moments, were likely driven by arousal.

It didn't matter. Just hearing him say those things was enough. And if it were possible to give him of her life to fill his needs, she would have surrendered it.

She surrendered what she could now, all of herself.

He swept her pajama top over her head, his arm beneath her melting her into his length, circling her waist, raising her against the headboard to bury his face into her confined breasts.

She moaned at seeing the dark majesty of his head against her, let her hands fulfill what she'd thought would remain a fantasy, burying them in the luxury of his silken, raven mane, pressing his head harder to her aching flesh.

He groaned something deep and driven, the sound spearing from his lips into her heart as his hands went to her back. She arched, helping him release breasts now peaked with arousal, throbbing for his ownership.

He gathered her hands again above her head, drew back to gaze at her. Naked to the waist, the image of abandon, on wanton offer. She turned her face into the sheets, unable to withstand his burning scrutiny.

"Look at me, *ya galbi*." His demand overrode her will, drew her eyes to his. "See what your sight does to me." He let one of her hands go, took it to his heart, let her feel the power of its thundering, then to his erection. "Feel it."

Her hand trembled as it fulfilled the ultimate privilege of feeling his potency. She stroked his daunting length and hardness through the heavy silk of his pants.

He undid the drawstring, slowly, maddeningly, holding her eyes as he guided her hand underneath. Her hand shook at touching him without barriers, couldn't close around him. But even with the nip of awe and alarm, knowing all this would soon dominate her, she reveled in his amazing heat, his satin over steel, the edge of anxiety making her readiness flow heavier, soaking her panties.

He came down over her again, thrust his tongue inside her mouth to her stroking rhythm, groaned inside her, "Your touch is a far better heaven than any I imagined."

She was lost in his feel when he suddenly drew back, spread her again, closed trembling hands on her breasts. She arched off the bed, in a shock of pleasure, making a fuller offering of her flesh. He kneaded her, pinched her nipples, had her writhing, begging, before he coaxed and caressed the rest of her clothes off her burning flesh.

The spike of ferocity in his eyes as they touched her full nakedness should have been alarming. It only sent her heart almost racing to a standstill with shyness, with anticipation. With pride that her sight affected him that intensely.

He tore his *abaya* off, finally exposing the body she'd known would make the gods of old fade into nothing. *"Ya Ullah ya Gwen, koll shai ma'ak afdal menn ahlami. Anti ajmal shai ra'aytoh fi hayati...anti rao'ah."*

Her awed hands shook over his burnished, sculpted perfection, barely biting back the protest that everything with *him* was better than *her* dreams, that it was he who was the most beautiful thing she'd ever seen in her life, he who was the wonder.

"Habibati..." His groan roughened to a growl as he rubbed his chest against her breasts until she thrashed beneath him. He bent, opened his mouth over her breasts as if he'd devour her.

Pleasure jackknifed through her with each nip of his teeth, each long, hard draw of his lips, had her shuddering all over.

"Fareed, just take me...all of me..."

He told her he wanted exactly that. All of her now. *Now.*
"Bareedek kollek, daheenah, habibati. Daheenah."

She lay powerless under the avalanche of need, her moans becoming keens as his surgeon's hand glided over her, taking every liberty and creating erogenous zones wherever they fondled and owned, before settling between her thighs. His strong, sensitive fingers slid up to her intimate flesh, now molten, throbbing its demand for his touch, his invasion. They opened the lips of her femininity, slid between her folds, soaked in her readiness.

It took only a few strokes of those virtuoso fingers to spill her over the edge. She convulsed with pleasure, hazy with it, failing to imagine what union with him would bring if just a few touches unraveled her body and mind.

Among her stifled cries of release she heard something primal rumble in his gut, knew it was the sound of his control snapping.

He came over her and her hands fumbled with his to remove his pants, the last barrier between them. She went nerveless as his lips spilled worship into hers, proclaiming her soul of his heart, his need to be inside her.

"Roh galbi, mehtaj akoon jow'waaki."

She couldn't bear not having him filling her, couldn't bear the emptiness he'd created inside her, couldn't... couldn't...

She *couldn't* let him take her when she hadn't told him...

No. She *couldn't* tell him. And she couldn't not have him. Just this once. She needed this once. It wasn't too much to ask, to take. She'd live in deprivation for the rest of her life.

And she sobbed her need, her desperation. "Come inside me, Fareed, now. Don't wait...just take me."

*"Aih, ya hayat galbi...*take me inside you, take all of me."

He bore down into her, as blinded, as lost. She cried out, in relief, in anguish, spread her legs wider for his demand, contained him, her heels digging into his buttocks, her nails into his back, demanding him, urging him.

His pained chuckle detailed his enjoyment of her frenzy as his muscled hips flexed, positioning himself at her entrance, prostrating her for his domination. Then in one burning plunge, he was there, inside her. Flesh in flesh.

The shock to her system was total.

Paralyzed, mute, she stared up at him, everything swollen and invaded and complete. He rested deep within her, stretching her beyond capacity, as incapacitated. Blackness frothed from the periphery of her vision, a storm front of pleasure advancing from her core. Fareed…at last.

It was he who broke the panting silence, his voice a feral growl now. "Gwen, the pleasure of you…*ya Ullah*…"

He rose on his palms, started to withdraw from her depths. She clung blindly, crazed for his branding pain and pleasure.

He withdrew all the way out, dragged a shriek of stimulation and loss from her. Before she cried out again for his return, he drove all the way back inside her.

On his next withdrawal, she lost what was left of her mind. She thrust her hips up, seeking his impalement. He bunched her hair in his fist, tugged her down to the bed, exposing her throat, latching his teeth into her flesh as if he'd consume her.

Then he plowed back into her, showed her that those first plunges had just been preparations. He fed her core more, then more of him with every thrust, causing an unknown, unbelievably pleasurable expansion within her, until she felt him hit the epicenter of her very essence.

She was destroyed, blind, mad, screaming, clinging to

him, biting him, convulsing, the ecstasy rending in intensity.

He withdrew, and she saw his magnificent face seize with ferocity, with his greed for every sensation he plumbed her body for, had ripping through her. Tension shot up in his eyes, as if he was judging when to let go.

She begged him, for him. "Give me—give me…"

And he gave. She felt each surge of his jetting climax inside her. It hit her at her peak, had her thrashing, weeping, unable to endure the spike in pleasure. Everything dimmed, faded…

She had no idea when awareness started trickling between the numb layers of satisfaction. She was still lying beneath Fareed. Then she realized what had roused her. He was leaving her body.

Before she could whimper with his loss, he pressed back over her, his weight sublime pleasure. She moaned her contentment. More bliss settled into her bones as he swept her around, draped her over his expansive body, mingling their sweat and satisfaction.

She closed her eyes, let his feel and those precious moments integrate into her cells. She'd need the memories to tide her through the rest of her life.

But this wasn't over yet. She had hours with him still.

She wouldn't waste a second.

"And I thought it would be unprecedented with you."

Everything inside her stilled.

Would his next words elaborate on the disappointment of his expectations? Had he given her her life's most transfiguring experience, but she'd proved no more than a barely adequate one?

Suddenly, she wanted to bolt. She wanted to hold on

to what she'd experienced. It would be all she had of him. And if it turned out to be a one-sided illusion…

"If I'd known how it would be between us, that it would far exceed even my perfectionist fantasies, I would have carried you off to my bed weeks ago."

She raised a wobbling head, trembling with relief. She marveled anew at his beauty, and at how magical their bodies looked entwined.

And she wanted more of him. Of them. All she could get.

She bent to taste the powerful pulse in his neck, dragging her teeth down his shoulder and chest to his nipple, nipping it before she moved her head up, stroking his flesh with her hair.

"I hope you know what you're inviting with this act of extreme provocation."

Feeling all-powerful with his desire, reckless with having nothing to lose and everything to win, before it was too late, she squeezed his steel buttock even as she slid her leg between his muscled, hair-roughened ones, her knee pressing an erection that felt even harder and more daunting than before.

"Which act are you referring to?" she purred, nipping his lips, adding more fuel to his reignited passion.

He grabbed her around the waist, brought her straddling him, menacing lust flaring in his eyes, filling his lips. "I have a list now. Each with a consequence all its own."

Her hunger, now she knew what ecstasy awaited her in his possession, was a hundred-fold that of her previous ignorance.

She rocked against him, bathing him in her arousal and their pleasure. "Terrible consequences all, I hope."

"Unspeakable." His hands convulsed in her flesh, raised her to scale his length. He dragged her down at the same moment he thrust upward, impaling her.

She screamed his name, body and mind unraveling at the unbearable expansion, the excruciating pleasure.

She melted into him, felt the world receding with only him left in existence. Along with one thought.

She'd had him. She'd been his.

Tomorrow, when she lost him, nothing could erase the experience from her body and soul.

Gwen had returned to her bedroom in the guest apartment as soon as Fareed had left her in bed. She'd hoped he'd stay away all day until she'd made her escape.

He hadn't stayed away an hour.

He'd just entered the bedroom, was walking to her in strides laden with urgency, something fierce blasting off him.

Before she could say anything, he hauled her into his arms and drowned her in the deepest kiss he'd claimed yet.

She felt his turmoil collide with hers, until she couldn't bear it, think of nothing but easing him.

She tugged at his hair gently, bringing his head up. And what she saw in his eyes almost brought tears to hers.

She'd seen this in his eyes off and on since they'd come here. This despair. Every time, being with her and Ryan had managed to erase the darkness that seemed to grip him heart and soul.

She'd never asked about the reason behind his anguish. Not only because she didn't feel she had the right to, but also because she thought she knew the answer. But what if she was wrong and there was some other reason? Something she could help with, at least by lending a sympathetic ear and heart?

"What is it, Fareed?"

He pulled her back, hugged her tighter, pressing her head to his chest, which heaved on a shuddering exhalation.

He spoke. And she wished she hadn't asked. For he told her, in mutilating detail, about his dead brother and the depth of futility and frustration he'd been suffering in his ongoing, fruitless quest to find his family.

"Then, a week after you came here, Emad found a lead that looked the most promising we've had yet. He's just told me it turned out to be another false hope."

Even had she had anything to say, the pain clamping her throat would have made it impossible to speak.

This was all her fault. And no fault of her own. She wished she could tell him to stop looking, to have mercy on himself, that he had nothing to blame himself for, had already done more than anyone would have dreamed. But she couldn't.

She could only leave and pray that in time, he'd end his search, come to terms with his failure, so that it would stop tearing at him.

Now all she could hope was that he'd go away again, give her a chance to leave without further heartache.

Before she pushed away, his hands were all over her, over himself, ridding them of their clothes. She knew the moment her flesh touched his, all would be lost. She had to act now.

She struggled out of his arms, hating herself and the whole world for having to say this, now of all times.

"I'm leaving Jizaan today."

He froze in mid-motion as he'd reached back for her, stared at her for a long, long moment.

Then his lips spread. In another moment a chuckle escaped him and intensified until he was laughing outright.

He at last wiped a tear of mirth. "Ah, Gwen, I needed that." He caught her back to him. "I love it when you let your wicked humor show, loved it when you teased me in bed. Teasing me out of it—if not for long—is even better."

He thought she was joking! And who could blame him, after the nightlong marathon of passion and abandonment?

He pulled her back into his arms and she gasped, "I'm serious, Fareed."

That made him loosen his arms enough so he could pull back, look at her, the humor in his eyes wavering.

She tried to maximize on her advantage, injected her expression and voice with all the firmness and finality she could muster. "With your follow-up of Ryan over, there's no reason to stay in Jizaan anymore. In fact, we should have left long before now. We've taken advantage of your generosity for far too long."

Devilry and desire ignited his eyes. "If last night has been your taking advantage of my...generosity, as you can *feel*—" he pulled her back against his hard length, his arousal living steel pressing into her abdomen "—I am in dire need for your exploitation to continue."

"What happened between us doesn't change a thing."

"Not *a* thing, no. *Every*thing."

She tried to turn her face away. "No! Nothing has changed or will ever change. We have to leave, Fareed. Please, don't make this hard. I have to—"

"I have to, too." He latched his lips on the frantic pulse in her neck, suckled her until she felt her heart pouring its beats and love into him. "I have to take you again, Gwen. I have to pleasure you again and again."

Then as she struggled to hold on to her sanity and resolve, he defeated her, practiced every spell of seduction on her viciously awakened body and starving heart.

She found herself naked, delirious with arousal and pleasure, straddling his powerful hips, her palms anchored on his chest as he dug his hands in her buttocks.

He held her by them, had her riding up and down his shaft, showing her the exact force and speed and angle to drive them both beyond insanity, egging her on.

"Ride me, Gwen, ride me."

Lost, mad, she obeyed him, rising and falling in a fever, milking his potency with her inner muscles, mines of pleasure detonating in her every cell.

It built and built. She rode and rode, faster, harder, her hands bunching in his muscles, her eyes feverish on his, her mouth open on harsh inhalations vented in frenzied cries.

When it became too much, she wailed, *"Fareed!"*

"Aih ya galbi, take your pleasure all over me. Take it." He crashed her down on him, forged to her womb.

She imploded around him for long, still moments, shaking uncontrollably as the tidal wave hovered. Then it crashed, splintered and reformed her around him, over and over.

He took over when she lost her rhythm, a convulsing mess of sensation, changed the angle of his thrusts, hitting a bundle of nerves that triggered a fiercer explosion. It wracked her, drained her to her last nerve ending.

Yet she needed more, him, joining her in ecstasy, begged for it.

This time when the world vanished and nothing but him remained, around her, inside her, she promised herself.

This *would* be the last time.

Or maybe another time when next they woke up. Or maybe just one more day. Yes, one more day wouldn't hurt. But after that, there would be no more. Never again…

114

Olivia Gates

Gwen(?)... she was more than... and more than... the man that... he would react...

Nine

Fareed gazed down on Gwen and thought this was what sunlight would be like made flesh, made woman.

Her hair gleamed and her skin glowed in the flickering light of a dozen oil lamps. He'd placed them around this bedroom with only her in mind. This bedroom that wasn't his.

After all the time he'd fantasized about having her in his bed, he'd picked her up that first night, and his feet had taken him here. A guest suite that had never been used before. He'd wanted them to have a place all their own, a place he hadn't been before, where all the memories would be of her, of them.

He leaned over her, his heart in a constant state of expansion. Her lips, slightly parted in sleep, were crimson and swollen from his possession. Just their sight scorched him with the memories of the past days. He bent and took them, unable to have enough. She moaned, opening for him, her tongue first accepting the caress of his own, then dueling with it, in that never-ending quest for tasting, taking, surrendering. Even in the depth of sleep, she couldn't have enough either.

He'd lost track of how many times he'd possessed her, how many times she'd claimed him back.

He pulled back, filled his sight and senses and memory with her, beyond his fantasies, lush and vital and glittering in the dimness, naked and vulnerable and the most overwhelming power he'd ever known. Her hold over him was absolute.

His love for her was as infinite.

He groaned as emotions welled inside him, debilitating and empowering, even as his body hardened beyond agony. He needed to plunge into her depths again, mingle with her body and soul.

His hand glided over her, absorbing her softness and resilience, the pleasure that hummed inside her at his touch, the craving echoing his. He caressed her from breast to the concavity of her waist, over the swell of her hips and the curve of her thigh. His hand hooked beneath her knee, opening her over him.

He savored her every jerk betraying her enjoyment, her torment, even as she still dreamed. He bent and took more suckles of the breasts that had rewhetted his appetite for life. She moaned as she spread her thighs for him, cradled him in the only place he'd ever call home, where the fluid heat of her welcome was unraveling his sanity all over again.

Her eyes half opened, heavy with sleep and lust, endless, insatiable skies. "Come inside me, Fareed...*now*."

He felt he now lived to hear her say this, to know how much he needed him, to join them in unbridled intimacy and abandon, to take every liberty and give every ecstasy.

He pressed into her, reveling in the music of her gasps, the intoxication of her undulations, the urgency of the hands that clamped his head to her engorged-with-need flesh, begging him to devour her. The scent of her arousal sent blood crashing in his head, thundering in his loins.

He raised his head to take her vocal confessions, poured his own. "Every moment with you, *ya roh galbi* is magic. I want everything with you, every contradiction. Right now, I want to be giving and tender and I want to be greedy and ferocious, all at once."

She clung to him, wrapped her legs around him, her lips feverish over his face and shoulders and chest. "You almost wrecked my sanity with your last session of giving tenderness. Give me greedy and ferocious, please. Please, Fareed, please!"

He'd never known there was such pride, such pleasure, as that her desire could engender. Now her urgency hit a chord of blind lust inside him, reverberated it until it snapped.

He snatched her beneath him, rose above her, his senses ricocheting within a body that felt hollowed. Every breath electrocuted him. Every heartbeat felt like a wrecking ball inside his chest. He wanted to tear into her, pound her until there were no more barriers between their bodies. And she wanted him to do it, to plunder her, was shaking apart for his domination.

But he'd give her even better. He'd give it all to her.

He unlocked her convulsive limbs from around his body, ignored her cries of protest, swept her around on her stomach.

She whimpered as he held her down, captured her mound. His fingers delved between her soaking folds to her trigger. She climaxed with the first strokes, bucking and shuddering beneath him.

He showed her no mercy, fingers gliding, spreading the moistness from her core, made her shred her body and throat on pleasure.

He kept stroking her, raggedly encouraging her to have her fill of pleasure, until she slumped beneath him. Then he plunged his fingers inside her, his thumb echoing the action on the outside. She writhed under the renewed stimulation; the need for release a rising crest of incoherence. She thrust against his hand until his *"Marrah kaman, ya galbi"* hurled her convulsing into another orgasm.

She subsided beneath him, a mute mass of tremors. His fingers remained deep inside her, started preparing her for the next peak.

"I swear, Fareed, if you don't take me now…I won't let you take me for…for…" She stopped, panting.

"Not finding a suitable length of deprivation?" He chuckled, removing his hand. "Because you'll also be depriving yourself?"

She threw him a smoldering glance over her shoulder, one that almost caused his already-overheated system to vapor lock. Then she purred, "Maybe there is another way out of this predicament."

She thrust the perfection of her smooth, slick bottom back into his erection. Sensation ripped through him on a beast's growl, making him lunge over her, snap his teeth into her shoulder, making her grind harder into him.

He ground back, whispered hotly in her ear, "I'm finding demonstrations far more effective than threats. Go on, give me examples of what you need me to do."

The look she gave him this time, the sight of her as she trembled up to her knees, her waterfall of sunshine and ripe golden breasts swaying gently, blanked his sanity, almost made him slam into her. But the need to have her seek him, relinquish yet another notch of inhibition, over-powered even the insanity.

She lowered her head and upper body to the mattress. The total submission in her position, the devouring in her gaze as she rested her face against the dark sheets and silently demanded his domination, sent his breath hissing in his throat like steam, his erection filling with what felt like molten lead.

He still needed more. "A superlative demonstration. Now I need accompanying directions of what's required of me."

And she gave him what he needed. "I want you to bury yourself all the way inside me, holding nothing back, until you finish me, send us both into oblivion."

The last tether of his restraint snapped so hard, he rammed into her with all the violence of its recoil, bottoming out in one thrust. A shout burned its way from both their depths.

"Nothing ever felt like this, Gwen," he growled as he thrust deeper, harder into her, feeling as if he'd delved into an inferno of pure ecstasy. "Being inside you, this fit, this intensity, this perfection. Nothing could possibly be this pleasurable. But it is, you are, more pleasure than is possible. You sate me and craze me with insatiability. You burn me, Gwen, body and reason."

She sobbed with every thrust. "You *burn* me, too…you fill me beyond my ability to withstand…or my ability to have enough. Oh, Fareed…the pain and pleasure of you… do it all to me…*do* it."

Feeling his body hurtling into the danger zone, he put all his power behind each plunge. She writhed beneath him, thrusting back, letting him forge new depths inside her, panting more confessions, more proddings. Pressure built in his loins with each slide and thrust, each word, spread from the point inside her he was hitting deepest.

He rode her ever harder, insane for her release, for his.

Then like shock waves heralding a detonation too far to be felt yet, it started. Ripples spread from the outside in, pushing everything to his center, compacting where he was buried in her. He took her, in one more perfect fusion, and it came. The spike of shearing pleasure, his body all but charring with its intensity, slam after slam after slam of spreading satisfaction.

He pitched her forward, filled her with his white-hot release as they melted into one being, replete, complete.

An eternity passed before his senses rebooted. He heard a hum, felt it, pure contentment rising from her as she received his full weight over her back. It made him wish he could remain like this forever, containing her, covering her.

It was beyond incredible, what they shared. Every time had the exhilaration, the voracity, the surprise of a first time, yet had the practiced certainty of a long-established relationship.

After moments, with utmost regret, he had to obey the fact that he was twice her size and weight, and that no matter how much she insisted she craved feeling his weight, practical issues like blood circulation and breathing still existed.

He slid off her slippery, satin flesh, turned her limp, sated body around, gathered her into the curve of his body, locked her into his limbs. She burrowed into him, opened her lips on his pulse, her breathing settling back from chaos to serenity as she sank back into contented sleep.

He sighed in bone-deep bliss. Having her pressed to his side, having her in his life was nirvana.

He couldn't believe it had been only a week since

they'd first made love. It felt as if he'd always gone to sleep wrapped around her and woken up to her filling his arms.

Yet one thing marred the perfection.

Even though he felt their connection deepening, she was only vocal, only demonstrative when it came to physical passion. And only when he aroused her beyond inhibition.

When he'd thought he'd resolved her withdrawal the day after their first magical night, he hadn't.

She'd woken up the next day with renewed desire to leave. He'd had to use every trick in the book of unrepentant seduction to make her relinquish her intentions.

He had, but only until the next day had dawned. She'd pulled back every morning, forcing him to recapture her each night. Then today, he'd come home running when Emad had informed him she'd been trying to arrange her departure from Jizaan.

That had driven it home that something serious was behind her persistence. But chiding her for trying to depart behind his back hadn't shed any light on that motivation, or obtained a promise that she wouldn't repeat her efforts. He'd given up trying, taken her in his arms, and everything had been burned away in their mutual abandon.

He still knew passion-induced amnesia would lift and she'd wake up pinched and troubled, and it would be déjà vu all over again.

But he wasn't worried anymore.

He'd finally figured out why she tried to limit their involvement to a passion with a daily-extended expiration date.

His lifelong experience had been with women who'd wanted him for his status and wealth. But for Gwen, the reverse was true. Even though she appreciated everything that he was, the man and the surgeon, the very things that attracted other women repelled her. She'd made it clear how vital to her equality in a relationship was. How deeply disturbed she must be at what she perceived as the imbalance of power between them.

But now that he knew the source of her agitation and aversion, he had the perfect solution in mind.

Feeling secure next morning would break the cycle of her daily withdrawal, he snuggled with her and closed his eyes, contentment blanketing him.

"You can't mean that!"

Fareed watched Gwen bolt up in bed, sighed. "Here we go again."

Gwen groaned. "Don't *you* start again, you know what I mean. But you still *can't* mean that!"

He stroked the gleaming tresses that rained over the peaked perfection of her breasts. "I can and I do."

She moaned as she caught his hands. "Don't, Fareed. This is out of the question."

"No, it's not. You're ideal, to say the least."

Exasperation rose in her eyes again. "You're just saying that because…"

And he turned serious. "Because I'm lucky beyond measure that the woman who blinds me with lust also arouses my utmost professional respect and satisfies my most demanding scientific standards."

She gaped at him, then groaned, "Don't exaggerate, please."

He sighed again. "Do credit me with *some* professional integrity, *ya roh galbi.*"

"Don't tell me you can't find anyone better to be the head of R & D in your new multibillion-dollar pharmaceutical department. A job that seems to have just become available now."

He shrugged. "It's been available for a while and no one satisfied all my criteria. You do. Your narrow field of expertise, your body of work and future research plans, all which made me attend your presentation those years ago, fit the closest with my own practice's best interests, and the center's overall focus." He ran a finger down her neck, between her breasts and lower. "What would you have me do? Look for someone less well-suited because you happen to be my specific libido trigger, too?"

She fidgeted in response to his words and touch. "Many would consider that a conflict of interest."

"I'd consider it a *conflagration* of interest. Beside this…" He caught her against his chest, groaned his delight as her lush breasts flattened against him, as her breath caught and her body heated again. "*I'd* get the most innovative and intrepid researcher in the field I'm interested in, while *you* fulfill your professional aspirations. Think what you can achieve, for your own career, for me and the center, for the world, with all the resources I'll put at your fingertips."

She still shook her head. "I—I can't stay here, Fareed."

He chalked one point up to his cause. She was no longer contesting the position itself, was down to the next worry.

"I know some aspects of the kingdom and culture are alien to you, maybe even disturbing. But many aspects delight you, too, and you've assimilated into much of your surroundings. And then I will never let anything negative affect you, or Ryan or Rose, in any way."

She bit her lip. He restrained his desire to replace them with his—he had to let her air her doubts so he could pulverize them.

She finally exhaled. "Nothing is really negative as much as it's different. But you and your family… I just can't get my head around how much power you wield here."

He'd been right. She was disturbed by the extent of his and his family's influence. She had seen the evidence of their almost absolute power in every aspect of life in the kingdom. "No one, including me and my family, will ever wield any power over you. You'll always be free to make your own decisions, personally and professionally."

"As evidenced by how I ended up doing everything you unilaterally thought was the only thing to be done?"

He cocked one eyebrow at her. "You're saying I coerced you?"

"I'm saying free will and you are mutually exclusive."

"I had to take charge of Ryan's care. Then I had to make you act on our shared desire. But if I ever feel that being with me is no longer your priority or good for Ryan, if you ever have a better offer professionally, I won't try to make you stay. This I promise you. On my honor."

She looked as if she'd burst into tears.

Before he rushed to add something, anything, she choked out, "Oh, God, Fareed…you're being so unfair. You're…deluging me with so much. But I have to say no. I never dreamed it would go this far, but if you're too blinded to care about your best interest, and ours, to end it *now*, I have to do it."

He wanted to kick himself. He hadn't considered those reasons for her reticence. That she believed he was compromising himself, and her, for something that would end. She was calculating the damages, to him, to her and Ryan, after such a finite, even if prolonged and powerful, interlude ended.

But he couldn't make it clear he had no intention of ending this. Before he discussed permanence, he had to first resolve all her issues, about her and Ryan's future here, give her more than offers and promises, show her how it would work in practice.

His cell phone rang. He ignored it, began, "Gwen, *galbi*..."

She grabbed his forearm. "Won't you answer?"

"No." He glared his annoyance at the phone on the dresser, tugged her nearer. "Now, Gwen..."

Her grip tightened. "That's Emad's ringtone."

He shrugged. "He'll call later. Gwen..."

"But he's not hanging up," she persisted. "It might be Ryan or Rose and my own phone is dead or something."

She scrambled to get out of bed, and he stopped her, resigned that the moment was ruined.

"I'll answer him." He jumped out of bed, reveling in her hungry eyes on his aroused nakedness, despite her alarm. "And it's *not* about Ryan or Rose, I'm sure, so you stay right there. I'm coming back as soon as I blast Emad to the farthest kingdom in the region."

He felt steam rising from his skin as he snatched up the phone and put it to his ear.

Emad preempted his frustration. "I need to speak to you."

"You couldn't have picked a worse time," he hissed.

Emad's exhalation was weary. "That's true, if not for the reason you mean. I am waiting downstairs in your office."

"I'll come down in an hour. Maybe two."

"No, *Somow'wak*." Emad sounded like never before. Blunt, brooking no arguments. "You'll come down *now*."

"Now" turned out to be twenty minutes later, the shortest time it took Fareed to dress and to take his leave of Gwen.

He strode into his office, displeasure roiling inside him.

"You'd better have some unprecedented reason for this, Emad..."

Suddenly, Fareed's blood froze in his arteries. The look on Emad's face. This was momentous.

This was about Hesham's family.

A lead had finally led somewhere. He could think of nothing else that would make Emad ask his presence so imperatively, or look so...so...

"You found them?" he rasped.

Emad gave a difficult nod.

Fareed's heart crashed. "Something happened to them?"

Emad leveled grim eyes on him. "No, but it's not much less terrible than if something had."

"*B'Ellahi,* Emad, just tell me," he roared.

Emad winced at his loss of control.

Then with regret heavy in his voice, he said, "I've found proof that Hesham's woman is...Gwen."

Ten

"You're insane."

That was all Fareed could say, could think. That was the only explanation for what Emad had just uttered.

"Her given name was Gwendo*lyn*. She changed it to Gwen in official documents since her college days."

A dizzying mixture of relief and rage churned inside Fareed's chest. "*That's* your 'proof'?"

Regret deepened in Emad's eyes. "That's just the tip of the iceberg. The doubts that made me investigate Gwen began when I became convinced she knew Arabic. She responded appropriately to things said in Arabic too many times, if only in that inimitable glint of understanding in her eyes, that I thought it strange she wouldn't mention it. So I tested my theory by speaking Arabic on purpose when she was within earshot and observing her reaction. She was careful not to show that she understood, but I could see that she did. I became absolutely certain when

I once calmly told a servant to walk out of the room naturally, then run like the wind to investigate the silent alarm I received from the southern guard post. Her alarm was unmistakable, and she tried to indirectly find out if anything was wrong. Because I spoke fast and idiomatically, I became certain she has knowledge of not only Arabic but our specific dialect."

Fareed rejected Emad's words as they exited his lips.

But another voice rose inside his mind, borne of the observations he'd never heeded. How she'd never asked what the things he said in Arabic meant, especially the endearments he deluged her in, how she seemed to respond appropriately...

No. She'd only understood his tone. He wasn't letting Emad poison his mind with his crazy theory.

Emad continued. "I couldn't find a reason why she'd hide her knowledge, but because I don't believe in inexplicable, yet innocent, behavior, I tried to get more information from Rose."

"*That's* what you've been doing with Rose?" Fareed growled. "Leading her on so she'd supply you with possible dirt on Gwen? You went too far in your efforts to 'protect' me this time, Emad."

"I was getting close to Rose for real, and I hope to get closer. Although I don't know how I will, with the truth revealed..."

"This is *not* the truth. All you have to support this insane theory is circumstantial evidence."

Pain etched deeper on Emad's face. "I have new evidence that the places where Gwen lived are also where Hesham lived, at the same time, that she now lives in the same town he did when he died. She seemed to be living alone in all these places, but then so did Hesham. They must have kept separate residences in Hesham's obsession to keep their relationship a secret. She became a free-lance researcher for the past four years so she wouldn't have a base. Then she left the job scene around the time she would have been in her last months of pregnancy and during Ryan's first months. She went back to work only when Rose became Ryan's nanny.

"And I didn't get any of that from Rose. She might be shockingly open, but only with her own opinions. She wouldn't have shared anything about Gwen. But she doesn't know much anyway because she lived across the continent with her late ex-husband for the last five years. They divorced years ago, but when he had a stroke that paralyzed him, Rose went back to take care of him. He died two months before Gwen contacted her and asked her to become Ryan's live-in nanny. Two weeks after Hesham died."

Fareed shook his head, repeated what looped in his mind under the barrage of information. "Circumstantial evidence, all of it."

Emad closed yet another escape route. "The one thing Rose mentioned was that a tragedy befell Gwen around the same time her ex-husband died. She wouldn't elaborate and I couldn't probe more than I did and have her suspect my motives."

"Good thing you couldn't afford to alienate the first woman to move your heart since your late wife."

"I couldn't afford to alert her to my suspicions and have her relay them to Gwen. If Gwen felt danger, we might lose Ryan."

"Now I *know* you're insane."

"I would give anything to be wrong, but with you being who you are, with what's at stake, I have to consider the worst possible explanation for her actions, until proven otherwise."

Fareed gritted his teeth. "Just to see what kind of twisted ideas you can come up with, what would said explanation be?"

"The ideas I have are courtesy of the twisted fortune hunters who've pursued you since you turned eighteen."

Outrage, on Gwen's behalf, boiled his blood. "And you somehow suspect Gwen is one of those, among everything else?"

"It's a theory, but it answers every question. She met Hesham in that conference…" At Fareed's stunned glance, Emad grunted. "Yes, I realized why I felt inclined to give her a chance. Seemed I recognized her but failed to place her. Until I remembered that you spent a whole evening staring at her across that ballroom."

So Emad had seen Gwen's effect on him that day. And Hesham *had* come to see him during the end-of-conference party.

He still refused to sanction any of the accumulating evidence. "So they were in the same place once…"

"And my theory goes that she realized you were related. Once you left, she might have approached him to ask about you and their relationship began."

Fareed groped for air. "That's preposterous."

"If you have a better explanation to fill the spaces in Hesham's story, I'd be the first to grab at it. But we can't afford to blind ourselves to what might be the truth. But if you find Gwen irresistible, Hesham, your closest brother in nature, would have found her so, too. It might have developed naturally between them, with the reason they met, you, unknown by him, and forgotten by her. Then everything went wrong and the king made his ultimatum, and Hesham went into hiding with her. Then he died and she walked away from the accident unscathed. Everything till that point could have been innocent and aboveboard. But

I hit a wall trying to find any good reason why she didn't come forward when you searched for her.

"With Hesham dead, from her perspective, the king's threat to her was no more. Without a legal marriage, or the possibility of one, making her and Ryan legitimate heirs of a member of the royal family, she must have realized she'd be beneath his notice, therefore safe. *But* she was also in no position to demand anything from the Aal Zaafers, apart from your own voluntary support. As lavish as that would have been had she gotten it, she might have wanted more. And she had the perfect plan to get it.

"She must have known how she affected you all those years ago, so she approached you incognito through Ryan's crisis. She could have used Hesham's knowledge of you to make you fall under her spell, to have not only all you can provide, for Hesham's and Ryan's sake, but all that you *are,* for hers. And she succeeded, didn't she?"

Fareed pulled at his hair, trying to counteract the pressure building inside his skull. "You're sick, Emad. I thought you liked her, thought…thought…" He stopped, suffocating. "You're *wrong,* about everything. She's not Hesham's woman."

Emad eyed him bleakly. "And if she is? Will you consider the rest of my explanations?"

"No," Fareed shouted. "Even if she is—and she *isn't*—she'd have a reason, a good, even noble reason for hiding the truth."

"You haven't asked her to marry you yet, have you?"

Fareed blinked. "What does that have to do with anything?"

"It explains her sudden persistence to leave. I know you've become…intimate, and she might have feared you might cool down. Threatening you with leaving might have been to push you to offer her what would make her stay forever."

"No. *No way.* She doesn't have one exploitative cell in her body. I don't need to know facts. I know *her.* And I reject your evidence." He bunched his fists, tried to bring his turmoil under control. "That will be all, Emad."

"Forgive me, *Somow'wak,* but I *have* to voice my worst fears."

Fareed barely contained his fury. "And you have. I will ask her. She will refute it all. I will believe her and *that* will be that."

"But we can't afford for you to confront her, *Somow'wak.*"

"Why wouldn't you want her to defend herself against your delusional deductions, except if you suspect they are just that?"

"Because if I'm right, confronting her would cost us Ryan."

"There you go again with this…*absurdity.*"

"It's anything but absurd, *Somow'wak.* I've marveled at the bond you forge deeper by the hour. Now I know you've both recognized the same blood running through your veins, the legacy of your most beloved sibling and his father. I'm certain part of your desire to have her is to have him, too. But she has full rights to him, and if any of the intentions I assigned to her were true, if she's exposed you might enter an ugly fight over him. One you're certain to lose."

Fareed felt he was watching an explosion, played in reverse.

Emad's revelations were the shrapnel hurtling back into place to re-form the bomb. Which might be the truth.

Not his macabre rationalization of Gwen's motives and methods. But that she could be...be...

He couldn't even think it. It would be beyond endurance.

But it would explain so much. Her wariness and resistance from the first moment, her distress when he'd asked her about Ryan's father, his reaction to Ryan—which had the texture of what he'd felt for Hesham, the many similarities that *did* exist between the child Hesham had been and Ryan.

Then came Gwen's continued emotional reticence, her persistent efforts to stop their intimacies, to leave...

The doubt Emad had sown felt like a virus replicating at cancerous speed, infecting his every cell and thought.

He couldn't survive knowing. He wouldn't survive not knowing.

He stopped again. He didn't want his steps to take him back to her. He'd always rushed to her as if every step separating him from her dimmed his life force. Now...now...

Now those remaining steps were his last refuge. They could be what separated him from finding out that he couldn't love her.

Emad had tried his best to dissuade him from taking those steps. His parting advice still cut into his mind, paring away every belief in anything good and pure, painting his world with the ugliness of manipulation and deceit.

Marry her. Without confronting her. Make her give you all rights to Ryan, secure Hesham's son. Then *deal with her, according to her innocence or guilt.*

His steps ran out. They'd taken him where he'd experienced his life's first true happiness, the consummation of his most profound bond. Where he might now end it all.

He opened the door, stepped inside. She wasn't there.

He'd have the respite of ignorance, of hope, a bit longer.

A vase swayed as he bumped into it. It crashed, broke into countless, useless shards. Just like his heart might moments from now.

A door slammed and footsteps spilled onto the hardwood floor.

She emerged from the chamber leading to the bathroom, half-running, the face of all his hopes and dreams, alarmed, concerned, sublime in beauty. "Fareed, what…"

She faltered as she saw the ruins at his feet, took in his frozen stance.

Then it was there in her eyes. The realization. The desperation. The fear. Of exposure.

Certainty flooded him, drowned anything else inside him.

She *was* Hesham's woman.

Gwen stared at the stranger who looked back at her out of Fareed's eyes, desperation detonating in her heart.

He'd somehow found out.

"Laish?"

"Fareed, please…"

They'd spoken at the same moment. But he'd finished even as she stumbled to find words to implore him with.

He'd said all he was going to say.

He'd only asked, *"Why?"*

Why she'd lied. Why she'd kept lying.

She could only ask her own burning question, "How?"

The stranger who now inhabited Fareed's body said, "Emad."

She had no idea how Emad had found out, where she'd gone wrong. He couldn't have gotten it out of Rose. She didn't know.

"This is why you kept pushing me away, insisting on leaving."

Statements. She could do nothing but nod.

She'd trapped herself the day she'd withheld the truth from him. And only sealed her fate when she'd grabbed at that one night with him and hadn't left right afterward, when she'd kept telling herself, just one more night.

"Ryan lahmi w'dammi. Laish khabbaiti?"

Ryan is my flesh and blood. Why did you hide it?

The way he said that, that haunted look in his eyes crushed her. She'd seen him in that videotaped request for her to come forward. He'd looked and sounded wrecked over his brother's death. He looked like that again, as if he'd lost him all over again.

She still couldn't tell him why.

But his eyes weren't only deadened with that grief she'd experienced for as long and as intensely. In them still lay his inexorableness. He'd have an answer.

She gave him all she could. "I was abiding by Hesham's will."

The moment she uttered Hesham's name, Fareed swayed like a building in a massive earthquake.

And if she'd thought his eyes had gone dead before, she knew how wrong she'd been. He now looked at her as someone would at his own murderer.

She couldn't survive his pain and disillusion. She had to try to alleviate them, with what she could reveal.

"I had to keep on doing what he did. You know the lengths he went to to hide his family's whereabouts and identity."

In that same deep-as-death voice, he asked, *"Gallek laish?"*

He'd always spoken Arabic unintentionally, to express his hunger and appreciation with the spontaneity and accuracy he could only achieve in his mother tongue. He'd usually been too submerged in passion to explain.

Now he spoke Arabic as if he was convinced she understood, wanted more proof of the depth of her deception.

Her heart twisted until it felt it would tear out its tethers. "He—he was convinced it would ruin his family to have... *your* family know of... our existence. This is why he hid. This is why I did, too. I—I only sought you out because of Ryan's problem, thought I'd get your opinion and leave. But things kept snowballing, then things between us... ignited, turning my position from difficult to impossible and I kept wanting to leave, to disappear, so you'd never know, never feel like this..."

"Too late now."

Silence crashed after his monotone statement.

She waited for him to add something, to restart her heart or still it forever.

He only said, "Tell me everything about the last years since I lost my brother. Tell me about your life with Hesham."

Gwen looked as if he'd asked her to take a scalpel to her own neck.

Fareed felt he'd be doing the same. Worse. That he'd be cutting out his heart. But he had to know. Even if it killed him.

He no longer recognized that dreadful drone that issued from him. "You met him in that conference?"

She cast her eyes downward. It was an unbearable moment before she nodded.

He felt as if a bullet had ripped through his heart, stilling its last jerking attempts at a beat.

He'd thought she'd recognized him that day, had ended her engagement because she couldn't be with anyone else.

All that time, it had been Hesham.

"Did you love him?"

She collapsed on the bed, dropped her face in her hands.

She *had* loved him. The grief he felt from her now was the same he'd felt at first. Her anguish for Ryan seemed an insufficient explanation, if that could be said. It had been due to the loss of Hesham, the father of her son.

And even though it shredded his heart, he had to tell her. "He loved you. He lived for you, and when he was dying, his only thoughts were of you. Even though he gave up his name and family and whole life to be with you, he thought you deserved more. His dying words were that he was sorry he couldn't give it to you."

Tears came then. Hers. He wished he could shed any.

He bled instead, dark torrents of loss.

Two things had been sustaining him. The hope of finding Hesham's family. And finding her and Ryan.

But they were one and the same, and his hopes for a blissful future for all were doomed to be forever tainted by the past.

It wasn't because he believed the ulterior motives Emad had assigned her secrecy. He wished he could. It would have been a far lesser blow to believe her a self-serving manipulator. He would have been relieved Hesham had died clinging to his false belief in her and at peace. As for his agony at losing his faith in her, it would have been ameliorated if he could have coveted her knowing what she truly was.

But she was everything he could love and respect, the answer to all his fantasies and needs. And that she'd been the same to his brother, had been his in such an abiding love that she'd become a fugitive to be with him...*that* was despair.

For even if he could survive the guilt—and may Ullah forgive him, the jealousy—how could he survive knowing she might never feel the same for him? What *did* she feel for him? Beyond physical hunger? Had he been unable to fathom her emotions because they didn't exist? Had she been unable to deny her body's needs, while her heart remained buried with Hesham?

If it had, had everything she'd had with *him* been an attempt to resurrect what she'd had with Hesham? Had she found solace in their minor resemblances, taken comfort in sensing the love he had for him?

Had she ever felt anything that was purely for him?

He had to get away from her before whatever held him together disintegrated.

He found himself at the door, heard himself saying, "I'll be at the center. Don't try to leave."

He couldn't make this a request. It could no longer be one.

Even if it would kill him, she was staying. Forever.

Gwen raised swollen eyes to the door that had closed behind Fareed. Heartbeats fractured inside her chest as she expected him to walk back, take her with him where he could keep an eye on her.

After moments of frozen dread, she tried to rise.

She sagged back to the bed. The bed she'd never share with Fareed again. In the apartment she'd realized wasn't his.

He hadn't taken her to his private domain, had kept her in what was to him, for all its wonders, an impersonal space.

Relief had trumped the pain of knowing he hadn't thought her worthy of sharing his own bed. She didn't wish the depth of her involvement on him, wished him only the mildness of fond memories when she left his life, not the harshness of unquenchable longing she'd live with.

But as he'd said, it was too late. Whatever he'd felt for her had now been forever soiled and soured.

It wasn't too late to escape. This time, she wouldn't let anything stop her. She'd at least spirit Ryan and Rose away.

Panic finally got her legs working. At the door, her hand slipped on the handle…then she stumbled back.

The door was opening. Fareed. He'd come back as she'd feared….

Next moment, she stood gaping at the stranger…*strangers* on the other side of the door.

The dark, imposing man who looked like the highest-ranking among them, advanced on her, said without preamble, "You will come with us. The king has summoned you."

The ride to the royal palace passed in harrowing silence.

Her escorts wouldn't answer her questions. They'd said the king had summoned her, but in reality, she was being abducted.

Even if she hadn't heard enough from Hesham about his father, this act of blatant disregard for her most basic rights made her expect the worst.

She'd long dreaded this man. Her fear only deepened with every step through his palace's impossible opulence and extravagance.

Then she was ushered into his state room.

As the door closed behind her, she felt engulfed by malice.

It didn't matter. She'd fight him, king or not….

"Harlots always had the intelligence and self-preservation to try to entrap my sons outside my domain."

The voice was pure wrath and mercilessness, short-circuiting her resolve. It issued from the deep shadows at the far end of the gigantic room.

The owner of the voice rose from a throne-like seat and advanced to the relatively illuminated part where she stood. She almost cringed. Almost. She wouldn't give him the satisfaction.

"But you're here to steal Fareed under my very nose. You're either recklessly stupid or unbelievably cunning. I'd go with the second interpretation because you managed to have my most-level-headed son eating out of your hand."

This was about Fareed? He didn't know who she was?

Relief almost burst out of her, but she couldn't give any outward sign of it. She stood staring ahead, face blank.

This provoked him even more. She felt his rage encompassing her as he stormed toward her. Then she saw him clearly for the first time. It took all that remained of her tattered control not to recoil.

The man was an older version of Fareed, as tall but bulkier, must have been as blessed by nature once upon a time, but ruthlessness had degraded his looks, turning him forbidding, almost sinister. And he was incensed.

"You think I'll lose another son to another American hussy? One who wants to foist her bastard child on him, too?" He snatched at her. Her heart hit her throat as she stumbled out of reach. He brought himself under control. "But I'll give you the choice I would have given the trash who deprived me of my youngest son. Leave, disappear, and I'll leave you alone. If you don't, what happens to you and yours will be your fault."

And she knew. That the lengths Hesham had gone to, to hide from that man, what she'd always suspected had been at least a little exaggerated, had been warranted, and then some.

But ironically, because of the king's ignorance of her

true identity, he was giving her a way out of this horrific mess. He'd even provided the means for her to leave against Fareed's will, what she might have never secured on her own.

"What will it be?" the king rumbled, a predator about to pounce and to hell with giving his opponent a running chance.

She looked him in the eyes, made her answer a solemn pledge. "I'll leave. And I'll disappear. Fareed will never find me again."

The king had believed her.

But knowing that Fareed wouldn't just let her go, he'd said he would give her every assistance in her disappearance efforts.

His men had delivered her to Fareed's mansion to collect Rose and Ryan on her way to the king's private airstrip. She'd phoned Rose ahead, told her to be ready, wouldn't answer her confusion.

She now ran into the mansion, had reached the bottom of the stairs when his voice came out of nowhere.

"If you're still trying to leave, Gwen, don't bother."

She stumbled with the force of the déjà vu.

Fareed was separating from the shadows at the top of the stairs like that first night he'd made her his.

God, *no.* Now this wouldn't be the clean surgical amputation she'd hoped it would be.

He was coming down the stairs now, as deliberate, as determined as that other night. But instead of the passion that had buffeted her then, the void emanating from him did now.

"I'm not letting you and Ryan go, Gwen. And that's final."

She took one step back for each he took closer. But

nothing stopped his advance. He was now mere feet away....

Then two things happened at once.

Rose appeared at the top of the stairs with Ryan. And the king's men, all six of them, who'd been waiting for her outside, entered the mansion in force.

Fareed swerved to advance on them in steps loaded with danger, putting himself between her and them, his expression thunderous.

"What's the meaning of this, Zayed?"

The man who'd led the task force that had taken her to the king gave him a curt bow.

"Forgive me for the intrusion, Prince Fareed, but the king has changed our orders. Only this woman and her female companion will leave the kingdom. The child, Prince Hesham's son, will remain—will be taken to him."

Eleven

"This woman and her child are in my protection."

At Fareed's arctic outrage, her gaze slammed from Rose and Ryan—frozen like her at the top of the stairs—back to him.

"My father is never coming near either of them. As for all of you, you will leave my house, right now, or suffer the consequences."

She'd never dreamed Fareed could look so lethal. And she knew. He would fulfill his threat without a second's hesitation. He was ready to fight, go to any lengths, inflict or sustain any injury, in their defense.

A chill of dread ran down her spine. She'd tried everything she could so that it would never come to that. But—No, she could have left sooner, prevented this. Now it was too late.

The king had discovered Ryan's identity.

The man called Zayed, what Gwen imagined desert

raiders must have looked like, harsh and weathered and unbending, stood his ground. *"Somow'wak,* by the authority vested in me by the king, I order you to stand aside."

Fareed barked a laugh that must have sent every hair in the place standing on end like it did hers. "Or what? You'll tell my father on me? Do so, and take this message back to that uncompromising fossil while you're at it, word for word. I'm not Hesham, and not only won't he intimidate me, but he also wouldn't want to make me his enemy. I will be if he even thinks of Gwen or Ryan again. And that's his first and final warning."

Zayed's face clenched in a conflict of reluctance and determination. It was apparent he liked and respected his prince, wouldn't want to fight him. But his allegiance, even if he didn't appear to relish it, was to the king, and it was unswerving.

He finally said, "My orders were clear, *Somow'wak.* I can't back down. *Arjook,* I beg of you, don't force a confrontation."

"That's exactly what I'll do, with anyone who dares threaten Gwen or Ryan." Fareed advanced on Zayed, a warrior who had the same steel-nerved precision and efficiency of the surgeon. "I'll go to war for them. Will you? Will he?"

She could feel Zayed hesitating as her mind churned, trying to work out how to exploit this standoff, take Ryan and Rose and escape them all.

But there was no way out. Either the king won, and she was thrown out of the country, or Fareed won, and he kept her here.

Either way, Ryan would end up being lost to her.

Suddenly, the simmering scene fractured.

Zayed made up his mind and gestured to his men. They advanced instantaneously, a highly organized strike force.

Two men ran past her and Fareed, targeting the stairs. She heard Rose's shouted protests and Ryan's alarmed crying as they advanced. Fareed intercepted Zayed and three of his men as they made a grab for her. She gaped in horror as violence erupted.

She cried out as a fist connected with Fareed's face, as she heard the sickening impact of knuckles with flesh and bone. And she threw herself into the fight, blind now but to one thing: defending him, preventing any injury to him at any cost.

Fareed took the man who'd hit him down with one blow to the throat and Zayed with another to the solar plexus. The third man he took down with one roundhouse kick to the temple. He was fighting with the economy of the surgeon who knew the anatomy of incapacitation. She hit and kicked the man she'd attacked, but he finally managed to restrain her.

Fareed turned on him, rumbling like an enraged tiger. "Take your hands off her, Mohsen, or have them torn off."

"*Assef, Somow'wak*—sorry, but you will stand aside now and let me complete my mission." Mohsen produced his gun from his holster.

She drove her elbow into his gut with all her strength.

He gasped, staggered, but he tightened his hold on her neck. She choked, the world wavered and receded. She heard Fareed's roar as if from a distance, saw his contorted face as he charged toward her and her captor, saw a gun pointing at him, from a hand beside her face. Dread for him swelled as she fought to sink her teeth into that hand...

"That's enough!"

A roar reverberated in her bones, then she was snatched from the vise imprisoning her, and swept into the arms she'd thought she'd never feel again in this life. Fareed's.

Her wavering gaze panned around. Emad was at the top of the stairs standing between Rose and Ryan and the men who'd gone after them, protecting them with his own body, like Fareed had done for her minutes ago. Fareed's guards were cordoning the scene, four or five to each of Zayed's men, pinning them at gunpoint.

"Took you long enough, Emad," Fareed snarled as he took her deeper into his embrace, beckoned to Emad to get Rose and Ryan down and into his protection.

"My apologies, *Somow'wak*." Emad led the shaken Rose who was clutching the bawling Ryan in a feverish embrace down the stairs, encompassing her by his side. Gwen bolted from Fareed's arms, reaching out to Ryan who threw himself in her trembling ones.

Fareed's footsteps almost overlapped hers, and the moment Ryan filled her arms, he took them both back into his own.

Ryan's sobs subsided as soon as he found himself nestled between their bodies, his arms around her neck but his face buried into Fareed's chest, recognizing him as their protector.

Emad went on. "I was on the road when I got your emergency signal. I had to investigate the situation and organize enough men and the plan to end this farce with minimum fuss."

"With *no* further fuss." Fareed turned his wrathful glance to Zayed. "Isn't that right, Zayed?"

Zayed, still trying to recover from the vicious blow Fareed had dealt him, looked at him with grudging consent, acknowledging that he'd outmaneuvered him, had won. This round. He gestured for his men to stand down, retreat.

In minutes, all armed men, the king's and Fareed's, had left the mansion.

Rose was the first one to break the silence that expanded after their departure. "Holy James Bond! What was all that about? And what do they mean Ryan is some prince's son?" Rose put her hand on Gwen's arm. "Is this true?"

Gwen gave a difficult nod, unable to meet anyone's eyes, hugging Ryan tighter, the fright still cascading through her in intensifying shudders.

Fareed tightened his arm around her, as if to absorb her chaos, squeezing the restless Ryan between them, crooning to him, "It's over, *ya sugheeri,* you're safe. I'm here and I'll always be here. No one is ever coming near you again."

A whimper caught in Gwen's throat at the protectiveness and promise in Fareed's voice, at the way Ryan responded. As if he understood and totally believed him, he transferred his arms from her neck to Fareed's, burrowing deep into him, his whimpers silenced.

She almost snatched him back into her arms, cried to Fareed not to promise Ryan what he wouldn't be able to deliver.

Before she could say anything, Fareed turned his eyes to her. "I'm sorry about what happened. My father will pay for this."

She shook her head. "It doesn't matter."

"Of course, it does. And it's partially my fault, *our* fault, my siblings' and mine. We've long become too involved in our lives and projects, we've left his council to work unopposed. He's always been old-school, and has grown more rigid with age. That had once proven effective in matters of state, but when his inflexibility started causing problems, we just fixed them, instead of fixing his views and policies. And we've been paying bigger prices for treating the symptoms instead of the disease. His last unforgivable action was what he'd done to Hesham. But today he's gone too far."

Her headshake was more despondent this time. "I meant it doesn't matter what you, or I, do now. He's found out about Ryan, and everything that Hesham feared has come to pass."

Fareed frowned down at her, the intense pain that seemed to assail him when she mentioned Hesham gripping his face.

He turned to Emad, his frown deepening. "What I want to know is how my father found out about Ryan." The accusation was there in Fareed's voice. But when the confession surfaced with equal clarity on Emad's face, it still seemed to shock Fareed to his core. "*B'Ellahi,* why?"

Emad exhaled heavily. "I had no idea he'd react that way, but…I'd do it again, *Somow'wak.*"

Fury overcame confusion in Fareed's eyes as he ground out, "And you have a sane reason for this?"

Emad held his eyes, his grim but unwavering. "Because I've known the king longer than you have, have seen different sides to him than what he shows his children. But you are pragmatic and emotional at once and have never given your status or its dictates precedence over your decisions, so you never try to understand his position. There are worlds between being a prince who's not in line to the throne and being a king. That is the loneliest place to be."

"And is this analysis of my father's character and position and your view of both supposed to make any difference to me right now?" Fareed growled.

Emad shook his head. "I'm not asking that you forgive, just that you try to understand."

Sarcastic disgust coated Fareed's voice. "*Shukran,* Emad. I can't fault my father for playing true to type, but

I have *you* to thank for this impasse. You're a sentimental fool and you romanticized that heartless relic."

Emad cast his eyes downward, as if realizing anything he said now would incense Fareed further.

But Fareed wasn't done. "Because you've run to him with your discovery almost the moment you made it, have you also been keeping him updated on my efforts to find Gwen and Ryan?" Emad just nodded. Fareed snorted. "I can't tell you how great it is to find out that my most trusted ally is also a double agent. And for what? The most misguided sentimental *crap* for someone who's never shown anyone the least sympathy." He stopped, his fingers digging into Gwen's shoulder, his arm tightening over Ryan, as if he was intensifying his protection. "And among all those fond memories of my father, didn't you store the one when he forced Hesham into exile? Apart from the vile threats to the woman he loved, you do remember what he thought of the 'inferior union' that would soil our venerable line? So, because you're the expert on my father's deepest emotions and motives, *b'haggej'jaheem*—what by hell's name does he suddenly want with Hesham's son, the child he disowned before he came into being?"

Emad looked as if he wouldn't answer that, at the risk of enraging Fareed even more.

Then he did, his eyes heavy, solemn. "I know you think the king cared nothing about Hesham, and I might never be able to convince you otherwise. But he cared too much. He never stopped looking for him either, and in the last year or so, I believe it was to call him home, find a resolution that Hesham would accept. Then Hesham died and remorse and agony almost drove him to the brink of insanity. Only knowing Hesham had a son, and the hope of finding him, has been holding him together. Once I found out who that son was, I couldn't hide Ryan's existence and presence in Jizaan from him."

Fareed looked at Emad as if he was seeing him for the first time, his eyes gone totally cold for the first time since she'd seen him. "And I hope you're happy with the results of your catastrophic misjudgment."

And even though Emad had caused irreparable damage, she couldn't help squirming, as she felt Rose did, too, at the intensity of Fareed's disappointment in him, at Emad's mortification.

After a moment of heavy silence, without looking at Emad anymore, Fareed said a curt, "Ready the helicopter."

Emad only gave one of his deferential nods and strode out of the mansion. Rose ran out in his wake.

Gwen clutched Fareed's forearm. "Where are we going?"

"Where my father can't find us."

She clung harder, implored, "He will find us, sooner or later, Fareed. If you want to help me, help Ryan, you'll help us disappear. If you don't, your father will take Ryan away from me."

His face turned to stone. "No, he won't."

Her desperation mounted as she felt his finality trapping her, dooming Ryan. "If I don't disappear, he will."

His eyes bore into her as he put Ryan down on the floor, gave him a few things to play with. "So you're proposing to do what Hesham did? But Hesham could only do that because he gave up his Jizaanian nationality, changed his name and was a freelancer who could continue to be an artist wherever he lived. You won't be able to do any of that and remain yourself or sustain your career. *You* won't be able to wipe out your existence. Now that Emad has enlightened me about my father's obsession with finding Ryan, I know he would only trace you and kidnap him.

I also realize that was why Hesham begged me with his dying breaths to protect you. He must have known our father was still looking for him, was afraid he would find you and take Ryan from you. But it doesn't matter that he has now. I *will* protect you, but I can't do that long distance. You have to stay with me."

She was shaking all over now, feeling her world slip through her fingers like water, and there was nothing she could do to hang on to it.

"But you won't always be around," she pleaded. "You can't. I stand a better chance of keeping Ryan from him if I'm on the other side of the world, not here, where he rules absolute. You didn't see how he treated me. I wouldn't be surprised if he had me…"

Fareed's dug his fingers into her shoulder, stopping her projection in its track. "Gwen, you have nothing to fear, I swear it. I will fulfill my oath to Hesham. I will protect you, with my life. As for my father, he won't even think of coming near you once you're my wife."

Twelve

Gwen didn't know what happened after Fareed declared that she'd be his wife.

Everything blurred before her as he led her to a helipad behind the mansion where a sleek metal monster awaited them with Rose and Emad already inside. He buckled her in the passenger seat and took the pilot seat after securing Ryan in the back with Rose.

She barely noticed that he flew them over the desert, then out to sea. It could have been minutes or hours later when they came upon an island. He landed in front of a house in the same style as his mansion, only much smaller, steps away from darkening emerald waters and a golden beach glowing with the last rays of sunset.

Emad took Rose and a sound-asleep Ryan upstairs, leaving her and Fareed alone. Fareed gestured for her to wait for him as he walked away to get engaged in a marathon of phone calls.

He now walked back to her, tall and broad and inde-scribable, everything she could love, his fists clenched in the depths of his tailored pants pockets, his eyes cast downward, his brow knotted, his face cast in the harsh-ness of dark thoughts.

Had she imagined hearing him say she'd be his wife? Or was this why he looked so troubled? Because he was regretting it, was preparing to tell her that he hadn't meant it?

He raised his eyes. Her heart clenched at what filled them. Nothing she could understand. He'd been always near, clear. Now he was as far, as unfathomable as the stars that twinkled in the sky framing him through the open veranda doors.

He exhaled. "I've arranged everything. The cleric and the lawyers will be here in a couple of hours."

Her heart stumbled through many false starts as she waited for him to elaborate. He just kept his heavy gaze fixed on her, as if he expected her to be the one with some-thing to contribute. An answer. An opinion. An accep-tance.

But of what?

She finally asked, "What…what do you intend to do?"

His jaw muscles bunched. "Whatever will keep my father at bay. Now I know his true inclinations, we will need every weapon to stop him. In our culture, a paternal grandfather's claim to a child, especially if he's an elder or a man of status and wealth, can trump even a mother's. My father's claim as king would be absolute without any foul play. I now understand that when Hesham begged me to find you, he hoped I'd find you *first,* so I would do this."

"This? You mean…"

"Marry you," he completed when she couldn't. "A mother can only gain power against a grandfather's claim if she's married to a man of equal status and wealth. My status might not be as lofty as his here, but my international status and assets are weightier. When I adopt Ryan, we'll have enough rights among us to outweigh my father's claim to him."

This was a dream come true.

And the worst nightmare she could have imagined.

Fareed was offering her marriage. But only because he thought Hesham had meant him to, to keep his child out of their father's clutches.

She'd already known she'd been just a lover to him. As intense as it had been, had she stayed at his insistence, he would have ended it sooner or later. He would have never offered her anything permanent. He would have never loved her.

She'd been grateful for that. She should be grateful now. For this proposal that would secure Ryan's future.

Even if it destroyed hers.

Fareed had thought he'd already hit rock bottom.

He'd thought he'd never know deeper misery than when he'd found out Gwen had been Hesham's worshipped lover, the mother of his child. Now he knew there were more depths to sink to. It seemed as long as Gwen was in his life, and that was now going to be forever, he'd never stop spiraling down.

He hadn't expected her to jump for joy when he'd mentioned marriage. But he'd thought even if her emotions weren't involved, that she wanted him, might welcome the idea of marrying him, at least see the benefit to her and to Ryan.

But it seemed nothing worse could have happened to her.

It seemed she'd suspended her grief in her gratitude

for him and relief over Ryan's cure. She'd plunged into sexual intimacies with him, but must have thought she'd been betraying Hesham's memory, and with his brother of all people. To ameliorate her guilt, she'd been promising herself she'd leave, and he'd never know. She might have thought that by disappearing and putting up with any subsequent hardship to protect her child and Hesham's, she'd atone for succumbing to her need to feel alive and desired again. It had all been bearable, as long as it remained temporary.

But now she'd found out it would turn permanent. She'd realized that the only way to protect Ryan was to marry him, Hesham's brother, when she'd been unable to marry Hesham himself. This looked as welcome to her as a dull knife through her heart.

He had to stop her punishing herself, assure her that he wouldn't be compounding her guilt.

His voice was as dead as he felt inside as he said, "I want you to know that I will never ask anything of you again. This is to give Ryan, and you as his mother, the Aal Zaafer name, what Hesham should have been able to give you, with all the privileges that you're both entitled to. This is also to give Ryan the father he needs, the only man on earth who'll love him like a true son."

He'd thought he'd seen her distraught before. But now, she looked as if her heart were fracturing, as if his every word crushed it.

He knew this pact would sentence him to a lifetime of deprivation, but he had to finish detailing it. "I'll give you the *essmuh*. In our culture, this means that you'll control the marriage. You'd be able to end it, if you so wish, without my consent. I'll also give you full power of attorney, giving you control of my assets. In case anything happens to me, I'll make a provision to circumvent our inheritance laws, so you'd inherit everything. If we're both gone, everything will be Ryan's. If he's not of age, anyone you choose would be his guardian until he is. This will make you as powerful as I am, will give my father no way to attack you even if I'm gone. As for our daily life, I'll be in Ryan's life however you choose me to be."

And he was done. Finished. She looked as annihilated.

He watched her sag to the couch, then turned around.

He heard a helicopter.

It was time to make this terrible pact securing Gwen and Ryan forever binding.

"*Zawaj'toka nafsi.*"
I give you myself in marriage.

Gwen droned the words, her eyes glued to the pristine white handkerchief. Her hand was clasped with Fareed's beneath it. The cleric had his hand on top of theirs as he recited the Jizaanian marriage vows and prompted their repetition.

Emad and a guard were their witnesses. Rose and Ryan were present, one crying rivers, the other giggling a storm.

Soon the brief ritual was concluded and the cleric documented their marriage. She watched him drawing intricate script that looked as if he was casting spells, in a huge, ancient edition, the royal book of matrimony. Then he invited them to sign their vows and the details of the holy bargain they'd struck.

Fareed looked as if he was signing away his life.

Sinking deeper in misery, she signed, wishing she could sign her own. If only he'd take it, she would have.

One of the female servants let out a *zaghrootah,* a shrill, festive ululation. Rose—who thought this was all real in spite of the irregular circumstances she was just beginning to understand—was highly intrigued and tried to replicate the sound. Ryan was delighted and did his own ear-piercing imitations. Gwen felt her head might split open at any moment.

Fareed looked as pained at the unbridled mood as *sharbaat ward*—rose essence nectar—was distributed to those present in celebration of the happy marriage. But he endured it all with a stiff smile. He was the one who'd organized it after all.

She wondered why? It couldn't be because he was treating this as a real marriage. He'd told her in mutilating detail not to expect anything from him. Except everything she didn't want, that was. His status, his name, his wealth, in life and death. His heart had never been on offer. His passion, his ease and humor were things of the past. She wouldn't even have his companionship. She could only expect his presence where Ryan was involved.

She would have preferred it if he'd been enraged and outraged that she'd lied to him all this time. At least those would have been emotions, something to make her hope anything he'd felt for her survived, even if wounded. But he'd just turned off, as if he'd never felt a thing, not even on a physical level.

He hadn't even suspected her motives for hiding the truth. Didn't doubt she could be hiding even more. He'd just accepted her announced reasons, then proceeded to trust her with the sum total of his life and achievements.

But that wasn't for her, as he kept pointing out. That was for Hesham's woman, for Ryan's mother.

He was now probably putting on a show for those present, so they'd spread news of their marriage's authenticity. All for Hesham's memory, for Ryan's future.

None of it was for her.

And if he knew the whole truth, she'd lose even the crumbs he'd been forced to give her.

* * *

Tranquil waves frothed on the shore, erasing the names Fareed kept inscribing in the sand.

Gwen. Ryan. Gwen. Ryan.

He felt as if his world had emptied of anything but them.

It had been a week since they'd come here. He'd been away only to go the center for a few hours a day. When he returned, he hadn't been able to stay away from either of them all their waking hours. He had nothing but those. Longing for her kept him up nights, his mind and body on fire. He'd only slake it inside her, in her passion. And that was forever gone, too.

He might have survived it if he hadn't known what it was like with her, the pleasures that had enslaved his brother before him....

His thoughts convulsed on a torrent of regret. Jealousy and guilt were slowly poisoning him. And he could do nothing but let the emotions corrode him.

But at least his objective had been secured. He'd called every favor he was owed worldwide, had thrown money and influence at every obstacle in his path, and he'd gotten Ryan's adoption finalized. Gwen had been stunned when he'd told her in the morning.

Then this afternoon, she'd come out of the villa for the first time with Ryan, followed him as he'd paced the beach.

What had followed had been an unexpected torment, a simulation of the times they'd spent together as the family he'd thought they'd been forging. A glimpse of what might never, probably *would never* be. But then, whatever spontaneity and warmth he'd thought they'd shared had had probably been both of them responding to Ryan's delighted discovery of his surroundings, his tireless demand that they join him in frolicking in the sand and sea. Left to her own devices, she'd probably avoid him for life.

She would have.

Suddenly her scent carried to him even over the tanginess of the open sea. He braced himself, hating his weakness, the molten steel of ever-present desire that poured into his heart and loins.

"Ryan is finally sand-free."

He turned at her breathless declaration. She seemed to be floating to him in a full-length dress the sunlit color of her hair. It molded to her, accentuating her willowy splendor as if made for her. Seemed he *could* translate his obsessive knowledge of her every dip and curve and swell to ultra-precise fit. It was one of the dresses he'd had delivered for her because she'd left her belongings in his mansion. He'd never thought he could buy a woman clothes. Visualizing, fitting and buying them for *her* could turn into an addiction. As everything concerning her had.

She stopped before him, her skin and hair reflecting the radiance of the setting sun, her eyes the endlessness of the sky. Her warmth enveloped him, her hesitant smile pierced his vitals.

Then she reached out, almost touched him.

He wouldn't be able to resist such a brutal test. If she touched him, he'd drag her to the sand and take her. And she'd beg him to do everything to her. Then after the mindlessness of abandon, she'd sink into that misery that had so baffled him, that he now understood. He couldn't survive that of all things.

He caught her hand in midair, his jaw, his whole being rigid fighting the need to drag her by that supple hand, crush her beneath his aching flesh, ride her.

He hurt. Inside and out.

She pulled her hand away, her smile as shaky. "You have sand in your hair. Ryan bathed us both in it."

He gestured to her glowing cleanliness. "You're sand-free."

"Took a lot of heavy-duty scrubbing. The sand here is incredibly fine, like powdered gold."

He bit back a groan as the images and sensation bombarded him. He could almost feel his hands running down the smoothness of her slippery body as he lathered her, kneaded her under a steady jet of warm wetness, as he drove inside her tight, fluid heat, over and over until she climaxed around him, singed him with her pleasure. Then he would rinse her, caress and fondle her, whisper to her how she felt around him, what more he'd do to her as he brought her down from the pinnacle of pleasure, had her simmering for the next ride....

He exhaled forcibly, trying to expel the encroaching madness. "I'm glad Ryan enjoys the beach. Activities on the sand and in the sea are the best natural form of physiotherapy for him."

She bit her lower lip, made him feel she'd sunk those white teeth in his own, in his heart. "I never even took him to the pool. I was afraid to expose him to physical stress because I had no way of knowing if I'd be harming him. So it was his first exposure to the sea, and as you saw, he went berserk with delight."

He had been as thrilled as he could be in his condition with Ryan's joy. "We'll come here as often as possible, then."

She gave him such a look, hesitant, anxious, as if asking him what was to become of them, what kind of life they'd have.

What *did* she expect? They'd come here, they'd be together everywhere, where he'd be Ryan's father and her parenting partner, but never again her lover. They'd never be a real husband and wife and just a simulation of a family.

B'Ellahi, why was she here? Trying to smile and make small talk and shake sand out of his hair? Did she think he could be her easy companion now as he shared Ryan's upbringing?

Or *was* she considering resuming their intimacies because they were now married, for worse or worst?

Would he want this, if this were what she was after?

No. He'd either have all or none of her, couldn't share…

"Fareed, there's something I need…I *have* to confess to you."

His focus sharpened on her. Her incandescent beauty was now gilded by the lights emanating from the villa. The spasm of sheer love he felt for her, the enormity of it, suddenly crystallized one irrefutable fact.

He was wrong. He had been wrong. About everything he'd felt or thought since he'd found out she'd been Hesham's woman.

What she had been didn't matter. What she was did.

She was the woman he'd loved on sight, the only one who'd ever aroused his unadulterated desire, possessed his unqualified trust and admiration. She had been a selfless lover to his brother, then as sacrificing a mother to Ryan. She'd been the best thing that had ever happened to him, too, his life's first absolute intimacy. And he had been willing to give up anything, risk anything for her. His assets, his peace of mind, his hopes, his life. He now realized he could give up even more. He would.

He'd give up his jealousy, that Hesham had loved her first. His guilt over loving her when Hesham no longer could. His anguish over surviving when Hesham was no longer there.

But maybe she was already meeting him halfway. With this confession she wanted to make. He gestured for her to go ahead.

"You didn't question the reasons I stated for hiding Ryan's paternity..." She stopped, her agitation mounting.

He had to spare her. "There was nothing to question. You were doing what Hesham would have wanted you to do. He lived in fear of our father finding him and spoiling his life and yours. He clearly knew what Emad did, that our father *was* looking for him, not in the way I thought, out of anger. When he knew he'd die, he knew if he ever found you, you could lose Ryan to the man who almost destroyed him. My siblings and I were lucky because we had our mothers, whom everyone called the lioness, the Amazon and the harpy, to fend for us. But Hesham didn't. His mother died giving birth to him."

Her gaze wavered. "Hesham said your father never let anyone mention her to him as he grew up."

Fareed exhaled another of his frustrations with his father. "It *was* whispered around the kingdom that she couldn't withstand him, being this artistic, ethereal creature. It did seem that our father was so furious with her for being different from what he'd wanted, then for dying, that he banned any mention of her. When he realized Hesham was turning out like her, he did everything to force him into the mold he thought acceptable for a son of his. Hesham was right to fear our father and to instill that fear in you. If Ryan had fallen into his hands, he would have suffered an even worse fate because Hesham at least had us, older siblings who'd done all we could to temper his autocratic upbringing. So I understand that you had to hide the truth with all you had. I only wish you'd trusted me. At least, trusted Hesham's decision to entrust your and Ryan's futures to me."

She grabbed his forearm, urgency emanating from her. "I trusted you with Ryan's *life,* with *both* our lives when I came to the land I feared most on the strength of nothing but my belief in you. But it's more complicated than you think. And when we...we..."

"Became lovers?" He placed his hand on top of hers before she could retract it. "I *can* see how this made you feel more trapped. But after I was furious with Emad when he revealed the truth, then told my father, I can't be more thankful to him now. Like we say here, *assa an takraho shai wa hwa khayronn lakom.*"

She nodded. *"You may hate something and it's for your best."*

He smiled. "I'll never stop being impressed by how good your Arabic is. Hesham taught you well."

She blushed. *Blushed.* With pleasure at his praise. And at the ease with which he now referred to Hesham, and the beauty of the relationship she'd shared with him?

Then her color deepened to distress again. "But Emad didn't find out the full truth. And when you know it, you won't find acceptable excuses for my half truths."

He took her by the shoulders. "No, Gwen, whatever you hid, I'm on your side, and only on your side, always."

The tears gathered in her eyes slipped down the velvet of her cheeks as she nodded. "Hesham said your father told him his life story when he was fifteen. He said he married three women, one after the other for political and tribal obligations, had children from each, sometimes almost simultaneously." Fareed knew well the story of his father and his four wives and ten children. He had a feeling she'd tell him things he didn't know. "But he didn't love any of them."

"It was mutual, I assure you."

Gwen winced. "Yes. Then he met Hesham's mother and

they fell in love on sight." Fareed's jaw dropped. *That* he surely didn't know. He believed his father was love-proof, let alone to the on-sight variety. "But even if his marriages were to serve the kingdom, she wouldn't be a fourth wife. So he divorced his wives wholesale, and dealt with the catastrophic political fallout."

He was only six when this happened. He still remembered the upheavals. "My mother and the other two women say it was the best day of their lives when they finally got rid of him."

She nodded. "It was how he convinced Hesham's mother to marry him. She feared if he could divorce the mothers of his children so easily, that she couldn't trust him. So he let her interview them and they told her it was what they longed for, how they, like him, had felt trapped in the marriages, that he'd never loved anyone but her in his life. He pledged only death would part *them*.

"Their marriage was deliriously happy, and when she got pregnant, he told her he'd love her child the most of his children. But she died, and he almost went insane. He at first hated the son he blamed for killing his love. Then as Hesham grew up and he saw her in him, he transferred all his love and expectations and obsessions to him. He ordered no one to mention her because it made him crazy with grief."

Fareed felt more disoriented than when his father's guard had struck him. "And it seems I will keep finding that I know nothing about those I considered my closest people."

She shut her eyes. "Th-there's more. Much more."

"Then *arjooki,* please, tell me everything."

She drew in a shaky breath. "What nobody knew is that a few years after Hesham's mother's death, her tribe, the royal family of Durrah, invoked an ancient Jizaanian law.

That if a king married more than one woman, the sons of his highest-ranking wife would succeed him to the throne, with no respect to age. Since Hesham's mother was a pure-blood princess, that made Hesham the crown prince."

He stared at her, beyond flabbergasted.

This…this…explained so much. Yet was totally inexplicable.

Not that he considered disbelieving her for a second.

But he had to ask. "*Kaif?* How could my father hide something like this? How is that not common knowledge?"

"Your father pledged to Hesham's maternal relatives that Hesham would be his crown prince. On one condition—that they reveal this to no one until he prepared his kingdom and his other sons, especially the one who lived his life believing he was his heir, for the change in succession. But most important, until he prepared Hesham for the role he'd be required to fill. They agreed, in a binding blood oath. The king told Hesham when he turned fifteen and your oldest brother, although still in confidence. Hesham said Abbas was sorry for him, if relieved for himself. He didn't relish being crown prince."

Fareed could believe that. Abbas was a swashbuckling, extreme-sport-loving, corporate-raiding daredevil. He dreaded the day he'd have to give up the wildness and freedom of his existence to step into their father's shoes. He always said, only half-jokingly, that the day of his *joloos* on the throne he'd turn the kingdom into a democracy and be on his way.

But it was making more sense by the second, explaining the infuriating enigma of his father.

"So this was why Father pressured Hesham to that extent. He was trying to turn him into the crown prince he knew he wasn't equipped to become."

"Yes, and this was why he so objected to…to…"

"To his choosing you. He must have had some pure-blood royal bride lined up for him, too. This does explain why he reacted so viciously to Hesham's news that he was marrying you."

"But even with Hesham gone, Ryan…"

"Wait, Hesham meant Ryan's name the way I pronounce it, the Arabic version, didn't he? But he picked it because it worked in your culture, too, with a different meaning."

She nodded, her urgency heightening at what she considered unimportant now. "What I was saying is that Ryan might still be considered the king's first-in-line heir. And this is why he might never give up trying to get custody of him."

He ran his hands down his face. "*Ya Ullah.* I see how your fear of our father is a thousand times what I believed it should be. But you no longer have to worry. Even a king's claim to his rightful heir wouldn't trump our combined custody."

"You might be wrong…"

His raised hand silenced her. Ominous thunder was approaching from the darkness that had engulfed the sea.

A helicopter. He would bet his center it was carrying his father. This had to be Emad's doing.

His fury crested as he turned to Gwen. "Go inside, please. I'll deal with this."

"Fareed, let me tell you first…"

But he was already running to meet the helicopter as it landed, needing to end this before it started. And to end Gwen's worries once and for all.

The moment his father stepped out of the helicopter that, to Fareed's fury, Emad was piloting, Fareed blocked his way.

"Father, go back where you came from. Gwen told me

everything. And it's over. Ryan will never be in your custody."

Challenge flared in his father's eyes. "I'm surprised you even think your 'adoption' is a deterrent. Our laws don't sanction adoption, just fostering, and adopting him according to another culture's laws means nothing."

"The deterrent is not only that Ryan has the Aal Zaafer name through me, not Hesham. It is that I'll give up my Jizaanian nationality if it will make my adoption binding anywhere in the world, starting with here. But most of all it is that I, a man of equal status to you and superior wealth, am married to Ryan's mother."

The king only transferred his gaze behind him. Gwen had followed him, was almost plastered to his back.

Then, without taking his eyes off her, his father said, "That is not your greatest weapon but your greatest weakness, Fareed. Gwen isn't Ryan's mother. She's his aunt."

Thirteen

Fareed heard his father's declaration. He understood the words. He couldn't make any sense of them.

Still looking at Gwen, his father addressed her this time, "It was your sister, Marilyn, who was Hesham's woman."

After all these months, Fareed had a full name for Hesham's Lyn. Marilyn. Not Gwendolyn.

He turned, no longer of his own volition, but under her agitation's compulsion.

She was looking at him, and only at him, her eyes flooded with imploring. Certainty was instantaneous, absolute.

She wasn't Hesham's woman. Wasn't Ryan's mother.

They would register. The import and impact of this knowledge. They would crash on him and rewrite his existence. But not now.

Now only one thing mattered.

He turned to his father. "It makes no difference. Ryan is Gwen's and you're not getting him."

His father's expression was one he well knew. A "you dare?" and a "dream on" rolled into one eyebrow raise.

Before he did something irretrievable, his father said, "I won't continue this discussion standing by a helicopter on a beach. Anyone would get the impression I'm not welcome."

"You're not," Fareed growled, aborting his father's stride. "And this discussion is over. There is nothing to discuss. And don't try to pull rank. You're not king here. I am."

His father ignored him, looked at Gwen. "And you're queen here. You won't invite your father-in-law into your home, even if your husband is rude enough not to?"

"Leave Gwen out of this, Father. I'm warning you…"

Gwen's hand on his arm stopped his tirade.

Then she stepped in front of him. "It would be an honor and a pleasure to receive you in o-our home, Your Majesty."

Fareed wanted to hug the breath right out of her, emotions colliding inside him. Pride and delight, at how she held herself, addressed his father, the effect her graciousness and classiness had on the old goat. Delight that she'd said *our* home. Oppression that she'd hesitated while saying it. But mostly, dread of letting his father deeper into their lives under any pretext.

He watched his father take Gwen's elbow as she led the way back into the villa. He walked a step behind, felt Emad fall into step with him. He only spared him a gritted "Later."

His father tossed him a glance. "Later, I might take him off your hands. It appears I've been remiss in estimating his worth."

"I'll make you a gift of him. It appears I've overestimated it."

Emad grunted something, the very sound of politeness. To Fareed's versed-in-his-noises ears, it sounded like a grown-up groaning at the posturing antics of two juvenile charges.

Once inside the villa, Gwen turned to his father. "We were about to have dinner. I hope you'll be able to join us. If you don't like seafood, I'll get something else prepared right away."

"The only time we met, I insulted and threatened you." The king's regard turned thoughtful. "Even if I abhorred seafood, it would still be better than crow."

Fareed blinked. Had his father just cracked a joke?

He could think of only one explanation for this aberration. He got his confirmation in Gwen's crimson discomfiture.

"Oh, no, you don't, Father. I'm damned if I let you play on Gwen's sympathies. You're not some kind, bereaved old man, so you can quit trying to blindside us into lowering our guard right now. We're not letting you get your hands on Ryan."

His father gave him a considering glance. "What have you told her I'd do when this comes to pass?"

"No 'when' here. And it was Hesham who told her—" he tried again to adjust to the fact that it hadn't been her Hesham had told, had loved "—told her *sister* that you almost loved him to death, pressuring and coercing and hounding him into becoming the heir you would find acceptable." Suddenly he couldn't stand not knowing. He swung his gaze to Gwen. "What happened to your sister?"

He knew the answer. If not from the fact that she had Ryan, then from the grief that he'd felt dimming her spirit. She'd been mourning her sister. How had she died?

He hated to resurrect her pain, her loss. But he needed knowledge to stop his father's incursion, especially now that he was using unexpected weapons.

He still almost retracted his question when mention of her sister reopened her wounds right before his eyes.

But she was already answering. "After the accident, they gave her only a preliminary exam. M-Marilyn was told she was fine. They discharged her to make room for those with obvious injuries. Hesham had already…" Her tears ran faster. "By the time I got to her she was deteriorating. I rushed her to another hospital, but she hung on only long enough to start my adoption of Ryan and give me her and Hesham's last will. I knew everything already because I more or less shared their lives, moving everywhere when they did. I stayed even closer after I realized something was wrong with Ryan…"

"So you *were* the one who diagnosed him."

A tear splashed on his hand, burning him through to his soul. "When he was four months old. But Hesham feared seeking you out."

He rounded on his father, snarling, "*That's* why you're not coming near Ryan, Father. Because Hesham feared you so much he wouldn't seek my help for his son, his own brother, the best-equipped to offer that help, until he was on his deathbed."

His father ignored his wrath, addressing Gwen directly. "But your adoption of Ryan hasn't been concluded yet."

Fareed felt his head about to explode.

It almost did when Gwen said, "It's still pending." That imploring that compromised his sanity intensified. "That's what I was trying to tell you. I expected you to find out when your legal team discovered I'm not the birth mother, and my adoption hasn't been finalized. But they somehow got *your* adoption approved without this coming to light."

His daze deepened. "I told them not to bother me with details, to just do *anything* to get my adoption through."

His father tsked. "Seems *anything* included falsifying data. Once a discrepancy is found, the adoption might be invalidated."

He erupted. "No, it won't. Go ahead. Do your worst, Father. I'm getting this fixed, and Ryan will be Gwen's and mine, legally, anywhere in the world, no matter what you do. I'll fight you, I'll fight Jizaan and Durrah and the whole world for him, for Gwen's right to be his mother. And I'll win. Ryan will never be anyone's but Gwen's, the one who loves him, who sacrificed all for him."

His father only sighed. "Have I ever told you how much I wish *you* were my heir?"

"You know better than to try to appeal to my ego, Father."

"No, you're right. What I wish is irrelevant. In matters of state, it always is. I hope Abbas will come around when it's time for him to take my place. He might not think so, but he'd make a formidable king. While you are more beneficial to Jizaan and the world being who you are, where you are."

"We're not talking matters of state here. I mean it, Father. I won't let you near Ryan."

"But it's not up to you." He turned to Gwen. "I would see my grandson now, *ya marat ebni*."

At hearing his father calling her "my son's wife," Gwen's eyes filled.

Fareed stopped her as she moved. "You don't have to."

Those eyes that were his world glittered with too much that they took his breath away. "He has more right to Ryan than I do."

"That's not true," he gritted. "You *are* his mother."

Twin tears slithered down her face as she tore her gaze away and hurried out of the room.

He stood glaring at his father as they waited for her to come back. She did in minutes, hugging a flushed-with-sleep Ryan.

At the sight of him, Ryan perked up with the smiles and sounds he bestowed on no one else. He was endlessly thankful for that, for he did love Ryan as if he were his own.

Then Ryan realized Gwen was taking him elsewhere and turned to investigate his new destination.

Ryan blinked and looked back at Fareed as if to make sure he hadn't teleported.

Fareed's jaw bunched. Surely Ryan didn't think he resembled his father *that* much? And even if they did share much of their looks, he couldn't possibly feel the same vibes from him!

Next moment, Ryan buried his face into Gwen's bosom. *That* was more like it.

Before satisfaction seethed inside Fareed's chest, he saw Ryan peeking shyly, inquisitively, *interestedly* at his father from the depths of Gwen's chest, and his tension roared back.

His father spoke, his voice rough with emotion, "*Ya Ullah,* this is Hesham as an infant all over again."

"That's not true," Fareed hissed. "Ryan is a replica of Gwen...of her sister, his mother."

His father turned to him with dazed eyes shimmering with what suspiciously looked like tears. "His coloring is throwing you off and that dimpled chin. But I am the one who hung on Hesham's every detail from birth. He has his same bone structure, the shape of his features. And wait until his hair grows out. It will be the exact color and curl as Hesham's. He'll also be like his father in many other ways. Isn't that right, *ya ebni?*"

Ryan squirmed excitedly in Gwen's arms as if he understood what the king was saying, and that he'd called him "my son." Then the king reached out to him, and with one last look at Gwen and Fareed, as if he was asking their permission, Ryan reached back.

Fareed's mind almost snapped when a tiny whimper escaped Gwen as she let Ryan go. He was about to snatch him back when her hand on his arm stopped him. He wouldn't have stopped if he'd seen dread filling her eyes. But what he saw there…it was something truly feminine, knowing, almost…serene.

He stood beside her, confounded, watched his father caress Ryan, murmur things for his ears only, what Ryan clearly liked.

When the introduction between child and grandfather seemed concluded, and they seemed to have come to an understanding, Ryan made his wish to be held by Fareed clear.

Fareed took him, feeling as if he was returning his own heart to his chest.

Silence reigned for endless moments.

His father finally let out a shuddering exhalation. "I have been more than half-mad since I lost my Kareemah." He looked at Fareed. "You might now realize how it was for me."

Fareed grudgingly had to concede that. If he lost Gwen…

He couldn't even think of it.

"Is that your excuse for what you did to her son and yours?"

"I thought I was honoring her memory, making her son my heir. But I wasn't sane most of the time. Not when it came to Hesham. He had too much of her, inspired in me the same overwhelming emotions." Suddenly his father seemed to let go of the invincibility he cloaked himself in, seemed to age twenty years over his sixty-five. "Now it's too late to right my wrongs. I'm the reason he's lost."

Gwen took an urgent step toward him, her eyes anxious, adamant. "You may be the reason for many things, but not that, Your Majesty. *Never* blame yourself for that. The accident that cost you your son, cost Fareed his brother and me my sister, was an act of blind fate. But I want you to know Hesham and Lyn *didn't* live in fear. While Hesham took hiding to unbelievable lengths, he and Lyn soon approached it all as an adventure, one they included me in. I never saw anyone more in love or delighted with every second they had together. The shadow of separation only made them appreciate every breath they had of each other. So in a way, you were to thank for the extraordinary relationship they had."

His father swayed and reached for the nearest chair, only to collapse in it, dropping his head into his hands.

Fareed stood frozen, watching this unprecedented sign that his father was human.

He finally raised reddened eyes, looking at Gwen. "I wish I could have met your mother, *ya bnayti*." Gwen started at hearing him call her "my daughter." "She must have been a remarkable woman to raise not only you, a woman who possesses such generosity, you'd offer me this absolution, this solace, after the injustices I dealt you and yours, but to raise *two* women who had my most fastidious sons think their lives are a small price to pay to have them. That was the kind of woman my Kareemah was. I hope she had a man worship her as she deserved, as I worshiped my Kareemah."

Gwen shook her head, her eyes as red. "Regretfully,

no. Our father took off while she was still pregnant with Marilyn. She raised us alone until an accident in the factory she worked in left her paralyzed from the waist down. She died from the complications of a spinal surgery years later, with only me and Marilyn with her. We changed our names to McNeal, her maiden name, because she was our only parent, our whole family."

Those were more shocking revelations to Fareed. More insights illuminating Gwen's life and character and choices.

"Your father had better be dead, too, or I will avenge her," his father rumbled as he rose.

Gwen started in alarm. "Oh, no. He's not worth it." Then she gave him a tremulous smile. "And then Mom always said it was the best thing that happened to all of us that he walked. She was happy without him. We were happy together. What happened afterward…blind fate was again to blame."

Fareed hugged her into him, unable to bear her losses, the gratitude that she'd survived it all, that he'd found her.

His father approached, his steps not completely steady. "I was only stating facts when I mentioned your pending adoption…."

Fareed cut him off. "Adoption or not, I will fight you, and I will win."

His father looked at Gwen. "Will you hold your dragon of a husband back?"

Gwen stared at him. Fareed did, too. A shaken king was unbelievable enough. An indulgent one had to be a hallucination.

His father exhaled. "I came here to negotiate, and that's why Emad let me come. But I won't now. Not because I believe you would triumph over me in any fight, Fareed. And not because I've learned a lesson I'll never recover from with Hesham. It's because seeing you together, talking to Gwen and meeting Ryan has changed everything. Gwen has given me a reason to live again with her forgiveness, on her own behalf and that of Hesham and her sister. I'm not losing this reason or more of my flesh and blood to the demands of duty and pride." He placed a hand on each of their shoulders. "You are Ryan's mother, Gwen. I will swear to that to the world, starting with the Aal Durrah. Ryan will be your heir, Fareed. While I only want to remain part of your lives, if you would have me."

Fareed gaped at him. He'd never…ever…

His stupefaction was interrupted by another surprise.

Gwen threw herself at his father, clung around his neck, reiterating, "Thank you, thank you."

His father was as taken aback. It took him long moments before he brought his shock under control and hugged her back.

At last he put her at arm's length, looked down at her. "You are all heart, aren't you? But you don't have to accept me. Your husband *can* get me off your backs permanently if he so wishes."

Her smile trembled up at him. "I don't want him to. And Ryan doesn't either. He wants his grandfather. He… recognized you, like he recognized Fareed."

"He was *far* more eager with me," Fareed protested.

His father *dared* placate him. "Of course he was. He knows his priorities, recognized you'd be the one who would be constantly present in his life and therefore in need of more intensive…humoring."

Fareed harrumphed. "With all due respect, Father…"

His father suddenly laughed. "I think you left it too late to even mention respect where I'm concerned, Fareed."

"Fine, we won't mention it. But even though I am thankful for your change of heart—make that flabbergasted by it, not to mention distressed that I have to revise my opinion of you, and of my whole life, and we do have to discuss the past, present and future down to the last detail later—please, *go away now*."

The king went away. Eventually. After the dinner Gwen had invited him to.

She was sorry she had. Not because it didn't turn out to be beyond her wildest expectations. It was because Fareed constantly looked about to explode with wanting him gone.

He didn't, thankfully, but he kept prodding him with demands to eat faster. He even cut up his food so he'd finish it sooner.

Now everyone was gone. She was alone with Fareed.

She wanted to do one thing. Beg. His forgiveness.

Before she found the words, he said, "Tell me. Everything."

Everything was made of one simple statement. "Lyn was with me during that conference party."

He looked at her as if he was revisualizing the past. It was as intense a gaze as what had mesmerized her during that conference. And changed her life forever.

"And Hesham was with me. I walked out, but he stayed behind, approached her."

She nodded. "I didn't notice much that night, but she told me later it was love at first sight."

"And the rest is history."

She had nothing to add. Not about this. But she had so much to say about everything else.

Words rushed under pressure. "I never dreamed your father could be this way. Hesham and Lyn made me dread him so much I…"

He waved away her explanations. "You had every right to expect the worst. I myself can't believe what happened

still, am wondering if he's biding his time until he can pull
something."

"I *know* he won't. But I wanted to be the one to tell you
the whole truth, and...I left it too late."

The weight of his gaze increased. "Why *didn't* you tell
me?"

She'd probably lose everything answering him. She
probably had already. But whatever happened, she owed
him a full confession. "I believed I'd just pass through
your life, and I'd be risking losing Ryan by revealing my
weaker claim to him, weaker than yours, let alone your
father's. I *did* trust you, but I thought if you knew, your
father eventually would. But I should have told you. You
married me because I didn't. I was still hoping that my
adoption would come through and the marriage would
serve its purpose. But we now know Ryan will be safe,
so the marriage no longer serves any purpose. Now you
can...end it."

His eyes had been flaring and subsiding like fanned
coals. Now they went almost black. "I gave you the
essmuh."

"Then...take it back."

"It doesn't work that way. Only you can end it now."

So this was it. Moment of truth. He would have never
chosen to be her husband. But he would remain in this
non-marriage for Ryan's sake or if she didn't release him.

"H-how do I do that?"

"You just tell me. The rest is just paperwork. It's the
words, the intention, that are binding."

She looked at him. The only man she'd ever or would
ever love. She'd be forever empty when he left her life.
But she'd be destroyed if she clung to him when he didn't
reciprocate.

And she let go. "I...end it."

* * *

Gwen closed Ryan's nursery door lost in dark musings.

Would he miss her if she left? Did he even need her anymore? Now that he had Fareed, his grandfather and an extensive family to love and cherish him? Or was she the one who needed him? He who was everything she had left to live for?

Fareed was probably realizing this now. That her role in Ryan's life had been as temporary as it had been in his. She'd protected him until she'd delivered him into the hands of those capable of giving him the love and life he deserved.

But knowing Fareed, out of kindness, he wouldn't say anything. He hadn't said anything as she'd given him back his freedom. But he must have welcomed it. Chivalry and honor aside, he'd probably welcome her disappearance from his life completely, would prefer not to have her in it through their connection to Ryan.

She approached the bedroom he'd given her. The one farthest from his. She'd hoped he'd cut her off from his passion because he'd thought she was his brother's woman, that when she confessed, his desire would be reignited.

But it had just been extinguished. The bad taste of her duplicity, however he mentally rationalized and accepted it, must have put out the lust that would have burned itself out sooner rather than later.

God, what was she still doing here? He no longer wanted her. Ryan no longer needed her. She had to go away now. She'd solve all their problems this way. She'd unburden Fareed of her presence, and Ryan was too young, he'd forget her in a month.

As for her, she might be less miserable without them, than with them and unwanted and unneeded. She might even survive.

She wouldn't if she stayed.

She opened the door, hesitated on the threshold.

What was she doing here anyway? She didn't need to gather her stuff. It wasn't hers in the first place. Nothing here had ever been hers.

She'd leave like she'd come, with nothing.

And this time, Fareed wouldn't come running to stop her. He'd stand by and would be relieved to see her go. He might even help...

"Do you know what I wanted to do when I saw you standing on that podium?"

Goose bumps stormed through her. The deep purr, like a coiled predator's, issued from the bed.

Fareed.

She grabbed at the light switch, her hand hitting and missing it many times before soft, indirect light illuminated him.

He was wearing an *abaya* again, both it and the loose pants beneath, white and gold trimmed this time. His hair gleamed wet and sooty from a shower, his skin glowed with the same bronze of the headboard he was propped against, with his legs stretched out almost to the end of the bed, crossed at the ankles.

He hurt her with his beauty.

What was he doing here? What did he mean when he asked...

His voice drowned everything again, answering his own question. "I wanted to walk up to you, gather your papers, tell you that you didn't need to solicit the world's approval or endorsement anymore, that you have mine, that I would put everything that I have at your disposal. Then I wanted to haul you over my shoulder and take you where I can ravish you."

She'd walked up to the bed. Was looking down at him. Was she dreaming this?

But he was saying things she hadn't even dreamed he'd say.

And he was saying more, infinitely better than any dream. "Then I discovered you were engaged. I was enraged, stunned. How could you not wait for me? I was also noble, *stupid* and I walked away. Four years of stoic deprivation later, you tell me you walked out of that conference and on that fiancé I fantasized about exiling to some undiscovered island."

His hand clasped hers, tugged her down. She fell over him, disbelief and debilitating relief racing through her. He melted her softness and longing into his hardness and demand. She shook, gasped, resuscitation surging from his every word and touch.

"Then instead of our siblings paving the way for our being together, everything they did kept us apart and it took a string of tragedies to unite us as we should have been from that first day."

He dissolved clothes that felt like thorns off her inflamed flesh as he spoke. She writhed in his arms, a flame igniting higher as he tore off his own clothes, the feel of his flesh her fuel.

He crushed her lips under his, breached her in a tongue-thrusting kiss that had her begging for his invasion now, no buildup, just total, instant possession.

He rolled her over, pressed his flesh onto her every exposed inch, driving her into the bed. "Then you were mine, then you were not, then you were my wife, but not really, then you set me free, when my freedom lies in making you mine, in being yours."

"You mean...you really wanted...this?" she gasped.

"Want is a flimsy, insubstantial emotion. Does it feel

like this to you?" He pressed the red-hot length of his erection, of every cabled muscle and sinew into her. Nothing flimsy or insubstantial there; everything invincible, enduring.

"I meant...you told me the marriage was only for Ryan, and to fulfill Hesham's last request."

"What would *you* tell the woman you were disintegrating for, if she looked like she was breaking up inside with grief and guilt, if you thought it was over your dead brother, and that she was hating you and herself for succumbing to your seduction and her needs? And when you're buried under misconceptions, would you tell her, and yourself, to get over that trivial matter of a beloved dead lover and brother, demand she be your wife for real?"

She gaped at him. And gaped some more. What he was saying...

Everything she hadn't been creative enough, daring enough, to hope for. His own version of her own misconceptions.

But one thing she couldn't get her head around yet. "You mean...you would have asked me to marry you... anyway?"

"Why so disbelieving? You wanted me from the moment you saw me, too. And you wanted me forever because it was how I wanted you. But I wasn't going to propose yet because I thought I first had to battle your issues with my family's clout and your fear of being a kept woman. Little did I know that, although those might have been considerations under other circumstances, you were only bound on sacrificing your heart for Ryan's safety."

She shook a head spinning with the revelations and re-alizations. "Fareed...I—I...can't..."

"Yes, you can, Gwen. Like you let me go, to be noble and self-sacrificing again, you can take me back. I'm giving you all that I am again, this time when you know it's all for you. Because I fell in love with you from that first moment, thought I'd be alone forever if I didn't have you."

"Fareed, oh, my love..."

He captured her hot gasp. "Say this again."

"I might never say anything else ever again. I've loved you from that first moment, too, knew that if I can't have you, I'd never want anyone else. Then..."

"Then everything happened. But we found each other again, and this, what we share, is worth every heartache we endured getting here, earning it. And even though Hesham and Lyn are gone, they left us Ryan, the most beautiful part of them. We'll continue to love them both in him, and he'll have us both to love."

"He...uh...might soon have more...people to love," she mumbled.

He stared at her. "You mean..."

She felt a flush spreading over her. "Too early to be sure, but...most probably." She hid her face into his chest, burning. "That's why I never mentioned protection. I wanted to have your baby, thought it would be all I had of you."

He turned her face up to his, his smile delight itself. "Same here." Then whimsy quirked his lips. "I shudder to think what more complications we could have had if we weren't already on the same wavelength."

She pulled his head down to hers, took his lips in a kiss that pledged him everything, melded them for life. "I'll tell you all I can think of. You. All of you. Your flesh in mine, your pleasure, your happiness, your existence."

And he joined them, took her, gave her, pledged back, "Then take all of me, for life, *ya hayati*. For you *are* my life."

* * * * *

PASSION

For a spicier, decidedly hotter read—
this is your destination for romance!

COMING NEXT MONTH
AVAILABLE FEBRUARY 14, 2012

#2137 TO KISS A KING
Kings of California
Maureen Child

#2138 WHAT HAPPENS IN CHARLESTON...
Dynasties: The Kincaids
Rachel Bailey

#2139 MORE THAN PERFECT
Billionaires and Babies
Day Leclaire

#2140 A COWBOY IN MANHATTAN
Colorado Cattle Barons
Barbara Dunlop

#2141 THE WAYWARD SON
The Master Vintners
Yvonne Lindsay

#2142 BED OF LIES
Paula Roe

You can find more information on upcoming Harlequin® titles,
free excerpts and more at www.HarlequinInsideRomance.com.

HDCNM0112

REQUEST YOUR FREE BOOKS!

2 FREE NOVELS PLUS 2 FREE GIFTS!

ALWAYS POWERFUL, PASSIONATE AND PROVOCATIVE

YES! Please send me 2 FREE Harlequin Desire® novels and my 2 FREE gifts (gifts are worth about $10). After receiving them, if I don't wish to receive any more books, I can return the shipping statement marked "cancel." If I don't cancel, I will receive 6 brand-new novels every month and be billed just $4.30 per book in the U.S. or $4.99 per book in Canada. That's a saving of at least 14% off the cover price! It's quite a bargain! Shipping and handling is just 50¢ per book in the U.S. and 75¢ per book in Canada.* I understand that accepting the 2 free books and gifts places me under no obligation to buy anything. I can always return a shipment and cancel at any time. Even if I never buy another book, the two free books and gifts are mine to keep forever.

225/326 HDN FEF3

Name	(PLEASE PRINT)	
Address		Apt. #
City	State/Prov.	Zip/Postal Code

Signature (if under 18, a parent or guardian must sign)

Mail to the **Reader Service:**

IN U.S.A.: P.O. Box 1867, Buffalo, NY 14240-1867
IN CANADA: P.O. Box 609, Fort Erie, Ontario L2A 5X3

Not valid for current subscribers to Harlequin Desire books.

Want to try two free books from another line?
Call 1-800-873-8635 or visit www.ReaderService.com.

* Terms and prices subject to change without notice. Prices do not include applicable taxes. Sales tax applicable in N.Y. Canadian residents will be charged applicable taxes. Offer not valid in Quebec. This offer is limited to one order per household. All orders subject to credit approval. Credit or debit balances in a customer's account(s) may be offset by any other outstanding balance owed by or to the customer. Please allow 4 to 6 weeks for delivery. Offer available while quantities last.

Your Privacy—The Reader Service is committed to protecting your privacy. Our Privacy Policy is available online at www.ReaderService.com or upon request from the Reader Service.

We make a portion of our mailing list available to reputable third parties that offer products we believe may interest you. If you prefer that we not exchange your name with third parties, or if you wish to clarify or modify your communication preferences, please visit us at www.ReaderService.com/consumerschoice or write to us at Reader Service Preference Service, P.O. Box 9062, Buffalo, NY 14269. Include your complete name and address.

HDES11B

*Louisa Morgan loves being around children.
So when she has the opportunity to tutor bedridden Ellie,
she's determined to bring joy back into the motherless
girl's world. Can she also help Ellie's father open his
heart again? Read on for a sneak peek of*

THE COWBOY FATHER

*by Linda Ford,
available February 2012 from Love Inspired Historical.*

Why had Louisa thought she could do this job? A bubble of self-pity whispered she was totally useless, but Louisa ignored it. She wasn't useless. She could help Ellie if the child allowed it.

Emmet walked her out, waiting until they were out of earshot to speak. "I sense you and Ellie are not getting along."

"Ellie has lost her freedom. On top of that, everything is new. Familiar things are gone. Her only defense is to exert what little independence she has left. I believe she will soon tire of it and find there are more enjoyable ways to pass the time."

He looked doubtful. Louisa feared he would tell her not to return. But after several seconds' consideration, he sighed heavily. "You're right about one thing. She's lost everything. She can hardly be blamed for feeling out of sorts."

"She hasn't lost everything, though." Her words were quiet, coming from a place full of certainty that Emmet was more than enough for this child. "She has you."

"She'll always have me. As long as I live." He clenched his fists. "And I fully intend to raise her in such a way that even if something happened to me, she would never feel like I was gone. I'd be in her thoughts and in her actions every day."

Peace filled Louisa. "Exactly what my father did."

Their gazes connected, forged a single thought about fathers and daughters...how each needed the other. How sweet the relationship was.

Louisa tipped her head away first. "I'll see you tomorrow."

Emmet nodded. "Until tomorrow then."

She climbed behind the wheel of their automobile and turned toward home. She admired Emmet's devotion to his child. It reminded her of the love her own father had lavished on Louisa and her sisters. Louisa smiled as fond memories of her father filled her thoughts. Ellie was a fortunate child to know such love.

Louisa understands what both father and daughter are going through. Will her compassion help them heal—and form a new family? Find out in
THE COWBOY FATHER
by Linda Ford, available February 14, 2012.

Love Inspired Books celebrates 15 years of inspirational romance in 2012! February puts the spotlight on Love Inspired Historical, with each book celebrating family and the special place it has in our hearts. Be sure to pick up all four Love Inspired Historical stories, available February 14, wherever books are sold.

SHLIHEXP0212

USA TODAY bestselling author

Sarah Morgan

brings readers another enchanting story

ONCE A FERRARA WIFE...

When Laurel Ferrara is summoned back to Sicily
by her estranged husband, billionaire
Cristiano Ferrara, Laurel knows things are about
to heat up. And Cristiano's power is a potent
reminder of his Sicilian dynasty's unbreakable rule:
once a Ferrara wife, always a Ferrara wife....

Sparks fly this February

Harlequin®

nocturne™

NEW YORK TIMES AND USA TODAY
BESTSELLING AUTHOR

RACHEL LEE

captivates with another installment of

The Claiming

When Yvonne Dupuis gets a creepy sensation that
someone is watching her, waiting in the shadows,
she turns to Messenger Investigations and finds herself
under the protection of vampire Creed Preston.
His hunger for her is extreme, but with evil lurking
at every turn Creed must protect Yvonne from the
demonic forces that are trying to capture her
and claim her for his own.

CLAIMED BY A VAMPIRE

Available in February wherever books are sold.

HN61876

Discover a touching new trilogy from
USA TODAY bestselling author

Janice Kay Johnson

Between Love and Duty

As the eldest brother of three, Duncan MacLachlan
is used to being in control and maintaining an
emotional distance; as a police captain it's his job.
But when he meets Jane Brooks, Duncan soon finds
his control slipping away. Together, they fight for a
young boy's future, and soon Duncan finds himself
hoping to build a future with Jane.

Available February 2012

From Father to Son
(March 2012)

The Call of Bravery
(April 2012)

HSR71758